DOCTOR·WHO

The Story of Martha

DOCTOR · WHO

The Story
of Martha

DAN ABNETT

with
David Roden,
Steve Lockley & Paul Lewis,
Robert Shearman,
and Simon Jowett

BBC
BOOKS

2 4 6 8 10 9 7 5 3 1

Published in 2008 by BBC Books, an imprint of Ebury Publishing.
Ebury Publishing is a division of the Random House Group Ltd.

Doctor Who is a BBC Wales production for BBC One
Executive Producers: Russell T Davies and Julie Gardner

Original series broadcast on BBC Television. Format © BBC 1963.
'Doctor Who', 'TARDIS' and the Doctor Who logo are trademarks of the
British Broadcasting Corporation and are used under licence.

The Random House Group Ltd Reg. No. 954009.
Addresses for companies within the Random House Group can be found at
www.randomhouse.co.uk.

A CIP catalogue record for this book is available from the British Library.

ISBN 978 1 846 07561 2

The Random House Group Limited supports the Forest Stewardship
Council (FSC), the leading international forest certification organisation.
All our titles that are printed on Greenpeace approved FSC certified
paper carry the FSC logo. Our paper procurement policy can be found
at www.rbooks.co.uk/environment

Series Consultant: Justin Richards
Project Editor: Steve Tribe
Cover design by Lee Binding © BBC 2008

Typeset in Albertina and Deviant Strain
Printed and bound in Germany by GGP Media GmbH, Poessneck

The Story of Martha

Transmission begins:

Space Lane Traffic is advised to stay away from Sol: 3, also known as Earth. Pilots are warned Sol: 3 is now entering Terminal Extinction. Planet Earth is closed. Planet Earth is closed. Planet Earth is closed...

It felt as if the whole world was made out of night.

Their small boat was running the tide inshore towards an invisible coast. Above them hung ink-black air, starless and heavy. Below them, the sea was as dark as the sky. It broke around the bows like black glass.

The little outboard motor chugged to itself. They were barely leaving a wake.

'The south coast grid can pick up a sonar echo at thirty miles,' one of the men in the shiny black oil slickers had told her when they embarked at Dunkirk. 'We'll be going softly, taking it slow.'

The two men in the shiny black oil slickers were Underground, of course. They were the last cell team to take up the tortuous relay that had conducted her from the Cursus Hill meet near the Orleans forage camps, around the Paris Crater, and then north through the burned fields of Picardy and Artois to Flanders, and the fortified sea walls and razor wire of the Channel coast. Like the smugglers of old, they knew the ways in and the ways out, and could navigate the darkness by smell and by touch: an old art, relearned. Sometimes, they even made it back alive.

The enclosing night was cool, and smelled of brine and Channel breezes. They'd waited at Dunkirk for two days, hoping for fog, but it was unseasonably clear, as if something was screwing with the weather patterns. Something, she thought, far more insidious than global warming.

In the end, she'd been the one who'd decided to go. Time was running out. The year was almost up. The stalwart men in their shiny black oil slickers had nodded. They would do their best. It was her, after all. So much depended upon her. As the year had gone by, she had acquired an extraordinary degree of fame that had begun to bother her. They treated her with a respect that bordered on reverence, as if she was some kind of legend or saint. She knew they would willingly die for her. She hoped it wouldn't come to that.

She sat on one of the wooden bracket seats, rocking with the motion of the little boat. Her leather jacket was buttoned up tight, and her nylon-weave rucksack hung heavily against her back. She tried to clear her head and prepare herself. She breathed deeply, smelled the sea salt in her nostrils, and stared straight ahead. The men in the shiny black oil slickers didn't speak.

The significance of their embarkation point had not escaped her: Dunkirk. Her kid brother, Leo, had been an enthusiastic reader of *Commando* comics as a child. She knew all about Dunkirk, and here she was, in a small boat, heading home despite terrible misfortune, ready to take a defiant stand against an apparently invincible enemy that believed it had already won.

There was so much to do, such vast odds to face down. The Doctor had trusted her, but she wondered if she was worth the trust. In her mind, she saw his kind, brown eyes, youthful and unchanged despite the age that had withered and creased his beautiful face. There had been perfect belief in them, a belief in her.

A year had passed since then. It had been hard, and there were parts of it that made her memory ache. She had endured every second of those twelve months. She had persevered. She had walked the Earth, and witnessed things that she would never forget: the islands of Japan on fire, New York in ruins, the poisoned Caspian, the frozen Nile, Shipyard Number One that had once been Russia. She had been through it all, and she had no way of knowing if her struggle had been anything like enough.

The year hung on her like a dead weight, and she dearly wished she could cast it off, erase it, dismiss it, wipe it out and start again, fresh. If only. If only it could be a year that never was.

That was a wish that couldn't be granted. The past year was real, and it was unchangeable. Most of her choices had been made for her, and it was up to her to do the rest.

It was up to her to finish it. It was up to her to save the world.

But how do you save a world that's already lost?

'Two minutes,' whispered one of the men in the shiny black oil slickers. She stiffened. The engine chugged.

'I don't see anything,' the other man hissed. 'There's nothing there.'

'Wait,' she said. 'They'll come. They have to come.'

The boat rocked under the blanket of darkness. The engine gurgled, idling.

'If they don't show,' said the first man, 'we'll have to turn back. You understand that? We will have to turn around. We can't stay out here, not even for you.'

She nodded.

'It won't come to that, Mathieu,' she replied. 'You trusted me once. Trust me again.'

He nodded. Even in the dark, she could tell his expression was less than convinced.

She didn't even believe herself.

A small, blue-white light appeared in the darkness ahead of them, tiny but stark. Once again, she was reminded of smugglers and the old days. It was a halogen lamp, flashing once, twice; a little cold star shining on an unseen beach.

'There!' she said.

The light began to swing, gently, from side to side.

Mathieu's comrade rose in the bows, and flashed his lamp back: two solid clicks.

They came in through the breakers, the outboard throbbing. She felt the boat's belly scrape and rumble across the shingle. Mathieu and his comrade jumped out into the water in their shiny black oil slickers, steadying the sides of the boat against the ebb. She got up and jumped out. Cold water sucked at her legs.

She looked back at the men wrangling the small boat. She couldn't see their faces. She wished she could.

'Make it right,' Mathieu said, out of the darkness.

'I will.'

'God bless you,' said the other man.

'I'm hoping we can settle this before it becomes a matter for God,' she said. 'Thank you, both, I—'

They didn't reply. They were already pulling the boat back off the shore, eager to turn around for France.

She ran up the beach towards the light. Her wet boots crunched over damp sand and pebbles. People had played here once. They had built sandcastles, licked ninety-nines, knotted handkerchiefs around their heads, and set up deck chairs and gaudy windbreaks.

She tried her hardest not to think about that. She turned and waved a last goodbye to the men in the shiny black oil slickers. They were too busy heaving the boat into the sea's back-splash to do more than half-raise their hands in response.

A young man was waiting for her on the foreshore, just beyond the tide reach. He held a halogen lamp in his hand. He was good-looking, tall, dark-haired and bearded, and he was dressed in fatigues. He watched her approach with a solemn, unsmiling face.

She came up to face him, slightly out of breath.

'What's your name, then?' she asked.

'Tom,' he said. 'Milligan. No need to ask who you are. Famous Martha Jones. How long since you were last in Britain?'

'Three hundred and sixty-five days,' Martha replied. 'It's been a long year.'

One Year Earlier

ONE

Travelling by vortex manipulator hurt. It hurt a lot. Martha hit the grass, rolling, gasping. Her sinuses ached. There was blood in her throat. Her organs felt like they'd been used as a boxer's speed bag. Captain Jack Harkness's teleport was right up there in the Top Five Worst Ways To Travel.

The instant before, she had been standing on the polished deck of HMS *Valiant*, the Master's airborne carrier base. She lay back on the damp grass for a moment, recovering her wits, remembering the scene. They had lost. They had lost everything. The Master had outplayed them at every step. The radio channels were frantic with transmissions of despair and astonishment. Jack had died at least once, Martha's family were prisoners, and the Doctor…

The Doctor…

Martha swallowed. She was determined not to cry. It served no purpose. It was weak, and the Doctor was trusting her not to be weak.

The Doctor…

The Master had aged the Doctor using a process built into his laser screwdriver. The Doctor had become old, very old – a helpless wizened shell. That had been, perhaps, the worst thing of all, to see the youthful, vital being she adored reduced to geriatric frailty. His eyes, his kind eyes, had cruelly remained young. They had stared at her fiercely, lost and hopeless, dismayed to find themselves imprisoned in a failing, infirm body that could no longer bound between stars and joke in the face of the impossible.

As the Master clapped and capered, the ancient thing that had once been the Doctor had leaned towards her, and whispered in her ear, just a few words. They were words Martha would never forget.

'We can't stop him,' Jack had gasped at her, coming back from the dead. 'Get out of here.'

With one last, hopeless glance at her mum, dad, and sister, Martha had triggered the vortex manipulator Jack had given her. She never ran from a fight, but she knew when a fight was lost. It felt like she was abandoning them, but she knew it was the only choice, not just for her mum and dad, or Tish or Jack, or even the Doctor, but for the entire human race. It was the only choice. If there was even a chance she could do what the Doctor had asked her to do, then she had to try.

Bang! One press of the manipulator, and Martha was Earth-side, rolling on damp grass, groaning in pain. She rose to her feet, unsteadily.

London lay before her. Like a blizzard of angry meteors, the Toclafane were hailing down, sweeping towards the city. The Toclafane were the Master's new allies. He had brought them here, by invitation. Metal spheres the size of soccer balls, the Toclafane sang as they swept in out of the clouds. Their voices were the voices of children, light, carefree, gleeful. Their wicked blades were out, their weapons flashing. Six billion cybernetic globes, singing childish songs of murder and malice, were descending on the Earth to exact decimation, as per the Master's unequivocal instruction.

Decimation. One in ten. One in ten must die.

Martha watched the flocks of globes rushing overhead, cackling and chuckling, zigging and zagging, zipping out searing beams of destructive energy. People, screaming and running in panic, burned to ashes as they dashed for cover. The park around her was littered with fires, and thousands of explosions pinpricked the London skyline.

Martha stood for a moment, stunned by the enormity of the Master's lethal tithe. Planet Earth was dying. The Toclafane were committing mass murder. She knew the same scene was being repeated all around the world. The human race was being culled, cowed and conquered. In a matter of minutes, Martha's species was being transformed into a cowering slave race.

She was determined not to cry.

Breathing hard, she glared up at the shoals of Toclafane sweeping overhead.

'I'm coming back,' she said.

TWO

Aleesha ran. She was nine years old. A flying metal ball had reduced her Aunt Charley to ashes, and when Charley's husband Grant had screamed at the ball, and tried to hit it with a rounders bat, it had incinerated him, too.

Aleesha had been staying with her aunt and uncle for the day. Her mum had gone up town to do some shopping. Her dad was out in Iraq, and sent letters when he could. Aleesha liked hanging out with Aunt Charley. Aunt Charley had a wicked sense of humour, and allowed Aleesha to play with the Wii even if there was still homework to do.

Aleesha didn't properly understand what had happened that morning. The sight of a flying metal ball making her aunt vanish was too improbable. She kept expecting Aunt Charley to appear from somewhere, laughing. 'Gone? Me? Not me, baby 'Leesha. It's like a magic trick.'

Aleesha knew that if her daddy didn't come back from Iraq, it would be because of something tangible like a bullet or a bomb. No one had told her that people could vanish like a puff of cinders – just like that! – if a humming ball hovered into the room.

The metal ball had spun in place, tilting, as if it was looking at her. Blades had flicked in and out of its casing. Aleesha waited, braced, for it to zap at her, but it had just rotated again and zoomed off out of the kitchen window.

Then Aleesha had run.

She had been running for two weeks.

The streets were mostly empty. There was no traffic. The skies, empty of planes from Stanstead and Gatwick, had turned beautifully clear.

Aleesha raided corner shops for chocolate and out-of-date sandwiches. She slept in empty houses and flats where the front doors had been left open.

Once in a while, some of the metal balls would zip overhead, laughing to themselves. Army trucks loaded with armed men grumbled past from time to time, but Aleesha avoided them, even though they reminded her of her dad.

There was nothing on the telly. She tried every set she found. The radio was dead too, tuned out to static. Hungry dogs, missing their masters, barked and growled in the back gardens of estates.

On the fourteenth day, chomping on a tuna sandwich from a plastic carton, Aleesha noticed how weeds had begun to flourish in lawns and flowerbeds.

She wondered how much longer her mum would be. How long did it take to go shopping up town?

***

Catford was no-go. The Unified Containment Forces had strung razor-wire barricades across the South Circular. There were sand-bagged machine-gun posts guarding the way in through Peckham.

From a flat in Deptford, Martha observed the Containment Forces through a pair of binoculars she'd liberated from a sporting goods store in Fulham: army types, mostly men, a few women, all dressed in black combat drills, all humping MP5s and waist-harnessed Glocks. They were the business. The Master hadn't been mucking about when it had come to recruiting. Martha wondered how much the Master was paying them. How was he paying them? What was he paying them with?

One thing was sure: Martha didn't want to face his private army. They were the kind of hard-marrowed killers who'd shoot on sight. They were the executors of Martial Law.

She slipped between them instead. Her key let her do that. It hung around her neck on a loop of string. The Doctor had made it for her, using a TARDIS key. They'd been eating fish and chips, her, Jack and the Doctor, hiding out in an abandoned warehouse. The key was a perception filter. It didn't render her invisible, just... inconsequential. The perception filter field generated by the adapted key allowed her to walk where she liked. People could see her, they just didn't really notice her. The filter blended her into the background.

Martha started. Gunfire, automatic fire, chattered a few streets away. The Containment Forces were at work nearby. Despite the protection of the key, Martha packed her things into her rucksack, and got ready to move. She had to find a new place to hide.

She felt safer when she was hiding.

'Hello, what's this?' asked Griffin. Rafferty slung his MP5 over his shoulder and turned to look where Griffin was pointing.

A high-end Land Rover had just swung into the street, flanked by two UCF outriders on BMW bikes. The Land Rover had been painted matt black, and UCF decals had been fixed to the doors.

'A potential pain in the backside, from the look of it,' Rafferty replied.

'Bowen, finish up!' Griffin called. 'Nice and tidy!'

'Yes, chief!' Bowen sang back. The squad was loading a group of dissidents into an open-back Scammell, ready to ship them off to the new labour camp in Bromley. They were a rag-tag bunch, miserably hunched, their hands on their heads. They jumped every time one of the squad team moved, or adjusted a weapon. Some of them were crying. One of them was nervously tapping his fingers against his thigh. Tap-tap-tap-tap! Tap-tap-tap-tap!

'Get into the truck!' Bowen shouted. 'I won't tell you twice!'

On the pavement in front of a newsagent's shop, six limp bodies lay under bloodstained sheets. *You have to make an impression*, Griffin believed. *You have to show these losers who's in charge. It's a new world all of a sudden.*

The Land Rover pulled up. The outriders halted, and put their feet down. As he walked towards the Land Rover with Rafferty in tow, Griffin could hear the bikes' radios chatter and pip.

A woman got out of the Land Rover. Like Griffin and his team, she was dressed in black combat drills. She was tall and good-looking, with short, groomed blonde hair.

'I'm looking for UCFA Griffin,' she announced.

'That's me, ma'am,' Griffin replied.

The woman looked at him, and they exchanged salutes. 'I'm ADC Dexter,' she said.

'I know exactly who you are, ma'am,' Griffin said. 'I thought the likes of you preferred to stay aboard the *Valiant*. Getting your boots dusty for a change, ma'am?'

'The likes of me?' the ADC sniffed.

Griffin shrugged.

'I don't mean nothing by it,' he said. 'How can I help you?'

The ADC pulled out a packet of sealed orders and handed them to Griffin. He tore them open and read them. 'Hard target search, UCFA Griffin,' the woman said. 'A Class Alpha dissident is suspected at large in this vicinity. Our Master wants her brought in. Your squad's assigned to this district, so you get the honours.'

'Lucky us,' muttered Rafferty.

'Martha Jones,' Griffin read. 'Who's Martha Jones?'

'A known associate of the Doctor,' the woman said. 'She's been on the run since Day Zero. Absconded from the *Valiant* by teleport.'

'She armed?' asked Griffin.

'Unlikely.'

'Dangerous?'

'Also unlikely. Our Master doesn't think she poses much of a threat at all, to be honest, but he's particularly edgy when it comes to all things Doctor-related. Martha Jones is a loose end that Our Master would like tidied up.'

'Begging your pardon, ma'am,' said Rafferty, 'but what makes you think this Jones woman is in this district?'

'It's all in the report,' replied the ADC. 'She used a teleport system to abscond, like I said. The *Valiant's* sensor systems have identified her set-down site: Handcross Park.'

Griffin sniffed. 'That's twenty miles away. And the fix is two weeks cold. She could be anywhere.'

'She's here,' replied the ADC. 'We've had several reports of her operating with dissident groups. Do a house to house, if you have to.'

The ADC turned, as if to leave. She paused.

'She'll be disguised,' she added.

'Disguised?' asked Griffin. 'What? Like a fake moustache and glasses?'

'She's using a perception filter,' said the ADC.

'And what's that?'

'It's hard to explain. She'll be tricky to spot. Hard to focus on. Your eyes will look elsewhere. Your mind will try not to notice her. Be alert. The moment you get a funny feeling, sharpen up. It'll be her.'

In the old days, Griffin would have laughed in her face. A perception filter? That sounded a little bit too sci-fi for his tastes, but things had changed in the last fortnight, and Griffin was open to a whole new world of wonder.

'This sounds like a job for the Toclafane, ma'am,' he said.

'The Toclafane can't read her,' said the ADC. 'This requires human senses.'

'If you say so, ma'am.'

'It won't be easy, but you *will* see her, because you want to see her. Our Master was quite specific. Walk with me a moment, Griffin.'

Griffin followed her away from the Land Rover and the waiting bikes. Behind them, Bowen was yelling at the dissidents for moving too slowly. The ADC smelled good in the warm sunlight. Griffin liked the smell of a handsome woman, even one in authority. At almost two metres, he towered over her, and his ex-SAS honed bulk eclipsed her.

'May I be candid, UCFA Griffin?' the ADC asked quietly.

'Candid as you like, ma'am.'

'Jones may have fallen into your district, but we're keen to have you work this for us. Our Master believes that you have training and skills that can be of particular use. He's reviewed your file, Griffin. He's taken a personal interest. He thinks you're the man for the job.'

'I'm flattered, ma'am,' said Griffin.

'And you'll be rewarded, Griffin. There's a chair opening up on the Sector Council. You pull this off, and I'll propose you myself. No more getting your boots dusty. You'll be a serious link in the chain of command. Besides which, you'll have come to the personal notice of Our Master. And that's how advancements are made.'

'I'll get right on it, ma'am,' Griffin smiled. His smile was not at all friendly, given the horizontal scar that split his cheek and lip, trophy of a Helmand Province tour.

The ADC nodded. 'This order supersedes all others. Hand off district duties to a subordinate. Form a kill team.'

'You want her dead, then?'

'Our Master wants her, period, Griffin. Hard target. I trust you won't be distracted by her good looks?'

Griffin looked at the order packet. 'She's certainly a pretty thing, ma'am,' he admitted, 'but you can trust me not to be swayed. Our Master only employs professionals.'

'Good to hear,' she said. She handed Griffin a mobile phone. 'Memory one is a direct line to me on the Valiant. Stay in touch. Keep me appraised. I'll do my best to give you all the support and back-up you need.'

Griffin looked at the phone.

'Our Master is really serious about this woman,' he said.

'He really is,' she replied.

He left Bowen to handle the snivelling dissidents. He drew out a core team to run with him: Bob Rafferty, his old oppo from Helmand; Lol Barker, an ex-para with a no-quit attitude he admired; Sean Jenks, another ex-para who'd seen service in Rwanda and Fallujah; Gordon 'Toffy' Bremner, a Royal Marine who'd done twenty months in Basra; and 'Yank' James Handley, an ex-USMC sergeant attached to the United States Secret Service. Griffin didn't know much about Handley's background. Handley had eagerly jumped into the Master's mercenary ranks when his principal, President Winters, had been assassinated by the Toclafane aboard the *Valiant* on Day Zero. Griffin reckoned that Handley wouldn't have made Secret Service without proper chops and, besides, Handley had killer eyes that Griffin had warmed to the moment he'd met him. Stone cold, grey, like wet slate. A man with eyes like that had to be useful.

They borrowed a UCF Humvee. Griffin held up the picture.

'Martha Jones,' he said.

'Sweet,' said Handley, with a whistle.

'She's proper easy on the eyes, chief,' said Rafferty.

'Contain yourselves,' Griffin snapped. He moved the photo aside, so it was out of their immediate vision.

'Still see her?' he asked.

'I saw her better when she was pointing at me, chief,' said Jenks.

'Get used to it. This'll be how it is. Sexy Martha is using a perception filter. You won't see her. She'll blind-side you.'

The men looked at him, waiting for the punchline.

'I'm serious,' Griffin said. 'She'll blend in. She'll be standing right beside you, and you won't know it.'

The men began to scoff.

'Shut up,' Griffin told them. 'This is why I picked you. You've all got the sense. The smarts. It's why you're alive today. You can all feel it when something's not right. I'm counting on that. This Jones girl is going to be hard to find. But if we do it, if we drag her in, dead or alive, mind you, then we will make Our Master seriously happy. Want your own island in the Med, Raff?'

'Thank you, chief!' Rafferty laughed.

'Want to be king of Africa, Toffy?'

'If the job's going begging, chief.'

'Want to be President of the United States, Yank?'

Handley smiled. 'I'd make a better fist of it than the last four clowns put together, Griff,' he chuckled.

'That's what this job could mean for us,' said Griffin softly. 'The personal favour for Our Master. Because he's master of the world, and he's asking us to do this. I'm not screwing around with you. This is the big one.'

The men growled their approval.

'Lol?' Griffin called out.

Lol Barker put the Humvee in drive and they prowled forward.

'Where do we start, chief?' asked Rafferty.

'I like your earrings,' said Aleesha.

'What?' asked Martha, coming to a halt.

'I like your earrings. My mum has some just like them.'

Martha stared down at the little girl. It was just getting dark. The vacant street and the empty houses around them felt all the more vacant as night closed in.

'You can see me?' asked Martha, smiling slightly.

Aleesha looked at her as if Martha had said something strange and grown-up.

'Of course I can. Why wouldn't I?'

'Well,' Martha began. 'I… Do you really think you should be eating that?' she added.

Aleesha looked down at the mouldy egg salad sandwich she had taken from the corner shop. 'Probably not. It's a bit yuck.'

'What's your name?' Martha asked.

'Aleesha,' Aleesha replied.

Martha bent down and faced her.

'You can really see me?' she asked.

'I can't any more,' Aleesha said, frowning. 'Why can't I? You're right there. I saw your pretty earrings. They were glittery.'

Martha took off the key and put it in her pocket. 'Better?' she asked.

'Oh yeah! I can see you, all properly. What's your name?'

'I'm Martha.'

'Hello, Martha, I'm Aleesha.'

'Hello, Aleesha,' Martha said.

'How did you do that, Martha?' Aleesha asked. 'Like… pop!'

'It's…' Martha began. She wanted to use the words 'perception filter', but she knew that would end up being too complicated.

'I wish my mum would appear like that,' said Aleesha. 'I keep expecting her to come back. Pop. I don't think she's ever going to come back.'

'Come on, Aleesha, of course she will.'

'I think she's ashes,' said Aleesha.

Martha took a quick, deep breath. She wouldn't cry, not in front of the little girl.

'Thank you, Aleesha,' she said.

'What for?'

'For noticing my earrings. I think I should take them off.' Martha began to wind the studs out of her ears.

She looked up. She'd heard the sound of an engine, a big engine. A UCF Humvee had just turned into the street.

Martha put the key back on and took Aleesha's hand. 'Aleesha?'

'Yes, Martha?'

'I need you to come with me. I need you to run.'

'I can do that,' said Aleesha.

THREE

'Did you see that?' asked Rafferty. 'Fifty yards down on the right. I saw something move.'

'So did I, chief,' Jenks told Griffin. 'It looked like a little girl. I think she went in through those houses.'

'I don't think she was alone,' said Rafferty.

'You see a second body?' asked Griffin.

'No,' said Rafferty. 'That's what I'm talking about.'

Griffin nodded. He checked the tactical log via the vehicle's dashboard PC. Over Watch appraisals reported a dissident group operating in the vicinity, but he could see the look on Rafferty's face.

'I saw the little girl, chief,' said Rafferty. 'I only realised there was someone with her when they were gone.'

'Go!' ordered Griffin.

Barker hit the brakes, and the squad dismounted. Safeties clacked off. They moved like shadows through the dusk, skirting abandoned cars.

Griffin prowled forwards. Half an egg salad sandwich

lay on the pavement, spilling from its plastic carton. Griffin raised his hand and made a series of quick gesture-commands. The men spread out. Barker led the way down an alley between the houses, his MP5 raised to his shoulder.

Griffin followed him. Could they really have got so lucky so soon?

Aleesha was keeping up pretty well. Hand in hand, they crossed a concrete yard edged by private garages, and then ran through a communal lawn area between three blocks of flats. A swing set and a miniature roundabout were surrounded by over-long, unmown grass.

Martha felt her heart racing. As the Doctor's travelling companion, she had experienced her fair share of dangerous escapades and close calls, but this was different. This felt unpleasantly real. The Doctor wasn't there to lift her spirits or explain the fantastical away. She was afraid. There were men with guns closing in behind them.

Martha was already beginning to despair over the mission the Doctor had sent her on. Two weeks since Day Zero, and she'd barely begun. She hadn't even left South London. She'd made ineffectual contact with a few groups of survivors, but they'd been too preoccupied with the day-to-day problems of finding food, water and places to sleep to pay her much attention. Martha was pretty sure at least one of the groups had given up info about her to the UCF in the hope of getting an amnesty.

Walk the Earth. Spread the word. It was just ridiculous. It was simply impossible. She was one woman. Her skills base did not cover urban survival or covert ops. She was learning all the time, but she kept making elementary mistakes. Sooner or later, something stupid was going to get her killed. Her earrings, for instance. Bright, shiny earrings. The little girl hadn't seen Martha, but she'd seen her earrings. Stupid, *stupid*.

Martha was pretty fit, but not fit enough for this kind of covert living. She'd been sleeping rough, sleeping badly, and her diet was lousy. She was tired all the time, and the little sleep she did get was populated by the Toclafane, the Master's smile and the Doctor's disappointed eyes.

They ran into the entrance hall of one of the blocks of flats. Martha pulled Aleesha in against the wall, and made a shushing gesture against her lips with her finger. Aleesha nodded, her eyes wide.

Martha snuck a look back. Outside, in the dying light, the communal court was empty. Somewhere, a famished dog was howling. A few, random street lamps, activated by light sensors, had begun to shine sodium yellow.

A man appeared. He was dressed in black and armed. A Containment Forces Agent. He edged out into the open, and came to a halt beside the swing set. He panned his automatic weapon around, then gestured. Two more men appeared, and then a fourth. They fanned out. The first man rested his foot against the recycled rubber seat of the swing and set it swaying, to and fro, on its chains. The chains squealed as they swung.

Martha knew she could find somewhere, hide, and let the perception filter do the rest, but she had the little girl to worry about. Aleesha didn't have a perception filter, and she certainly wasn't bullet-proof. Martha couldn't just leave her.

Aleesha had already been left, in the worst way. Martha wondered how long Aleesha had been waiting for her mum. The little girl might have been on her own for as long as two weeks.

That thought brought hot tears up in Martha's eyes. She breathed hard. She refused to cry. She absolutely wouldn't cry.

She wondered if she wanted to cry for Aleesha, for the Doctor, for the world… or just for herself, for being so useless. He should never have trusted her. She almost hated the Doctor for asking so much of her.

The UCF agent by the swing set turned, as if he had sensed her deep intake of breath, or had smelled her tears. He gestured and pointed. The men closed in around him and jogged towards the block of flats. There were six of them now.

'Up,' Martha whispered in Aleesha's ear. As quietly as they could, they ran up a flight of concrete steps into the base level of the tower block. The grubby stairwell led away above them, but to the left was an arch of twilight, an access way onto an upper court.

Martha gripped Aleesha's hand firmly and led her through the arch onto the court. Aleesha's trainers made no noise, but Martha's heels clacked. Stupid, *stupid*!

She stopped, pulled them off, and ran with Aleesha, in her socks, towards the neighbouring block.

They weren't going to make it all the way. The upper court, with its raised flowerbeds and skateboard ramps, was too wide to cross in one go with the men behind her. Martha dragged Aleesha into cover behind some wheelie bins. They hid.

Hiding, Martha thought, *is what I've spent most of the last two weeks doing.*

The howling dog was nearby. It had become frantic, perhaps picking up their scent. Martha and Aleesha cowered behind the foul-smelling bins.

The men appeared, fanning up onto the court, weapons raised. They exchanged gestures, nods, and shakes of heads. They spread out.

Martha knew they were going to find her and kill her. Worse still, they were going to kill a little girl who was only in this fix because she'd seen Martha's earrings. A grown woman and a little girl: just a meaningless footnote to the awful catalogue of deaths recorded in the last fortnight. Just two more names on a list no one would ever care to read.

Martha took a deep breath. She was totally, strangely focused. She wasn't going to allow this tiny crime to happen. The Doctor had trusted her. He had *trusted* her.

'Stay here,' she whispered to Aleesha.

'Where are you going?' Aleesha whispered back in great alarm. She wasn't about to allow the only adult who had noticed her in two weeks to go away.

'I'll be right back,' Martha whispered, 'but I need you to stay here, and hide. Can you do that?'

Aleesha nodded, and then said, 'Don't go.'

'Could you look after my shoes, Aleesha?' Martha whispered. 'Could you? And my earrings?'

Aleesha nodded again. Martha handed her shoes and earrings to the little girl. Aleesha closed her fist tight around the glittery studs.

'Stay here,' Martha whispered firmly.

She got up. The UCF agents had spread out wider across the court area. Martha could smell their sweat and the oil of their guns. Checking her key, she stepped out from behind the bins.

'Someone's here, chief,' said Bremner.

'I know it,' replied Griffin, circling on the spot, his weapon raised. 'Stay alert.'

Padding forwards, Martha crossed between two of the wary men. They didn't seem to see her.

She slipped behind another of the men, the one the other gunman had referred to as 'chief'. He was the biggest of them, with a memorable scar across his face. If she could get past him, and reach the other side of the court, Martha intended to make some kind of noise, cause a distraction, anything to lead the men away from the little girl.

She took another step.

'You smell that?' asked Jenks.

'What?' asked Rafferty.

'Perfume. That's perfume. A real sexy girl number,' Jenks said.

Griffin shook his head.

'I smell it, chief,' said Bremner.

Griffin narrowed his eyes. 'She's right here.'

Martha froze. She was out in the open. They were going to see her.

The man with the scar began to turn around.

There was a sound of breaking glass from the neighbouring block.

'Go!' Griffin yelled, and the men ran.

Left behind, Martha sucked in a huge breath and ran back to Aleesha.

The little girl was still clutching Martha's shoes.

'Come on!' Martha said, gripping her hand.

Griffin's team scrambled up the stairwell of the tower block.

'Second floor!' Griffin yelled.

They started to smash open doors, aiming weapons. There was movement behind the fourth door they kicked down. Jenks and Handley opened up. The automatic fire splintered the door frame and shredded furniture inside the flat.

'Cease! Cease fire!' Griffin yelled.

'It's just a dog!' Rafferty blurted. Just a dog, famished, trapped in the flat. The dog had somehow managed to overturn a DVD stand, which had broken the balcony window.

The gunfire had missed it. It was cowering, whining, behind the shot-up sofa, covered in flecks of upholstery padding and chips of glass.

'Damn, I was so sure we had her,' Griffin murmured. He knelt down beside the dog and stroked its head. 'Easy now, easy now, boy. That's it. Yeah, that's it.'

Petting the whimpering animal, Griffin unholstered his Glock.

***

Martha and Aleesha heard the pistol shot ring out over the court. They fled back the way they had come, across the street where the big Humvee was parked, and then down a breeze-way behind another residential block. They kept going until, five streets away, they couldn't run any more.

Panting, Martha picked a basement flat with an open front door. They darted down the steps from the street. Martha bolted the door and put the chain on. She smiled at Aleesha and winked. It took some effort to smile for the little girl's benefit.

'We'll be safe here for now,' she said.

Aleesha nodded, but she was clearly scared. Martha began to search around the flat for food or anything else they could use.

'I know you're frightened,' she said, 'but it's going to be all right. We will get through this.'

'Will we?' asked Aleesha. In two lonely, scary weeks, Aleesha had seen no evidence that anything was going to be all right.

Martha realised that the little girl was really shaken. She sat down beside her on the settee and took her hand.

'I tell you what, Aleesha,' Martha said gently, 'Would you like to hear a story?'

'Yes, please,' said Aleesha.

The Weeping

The storm screamed in across the frozen sea, its howling throat full of snow. As night began to yield to a sickly grey dawn it settled over the desolate city. And, yet, through the brutal roar of the storm another sound could be heard, distant, desolate and chilling. A broken-hearted howl which reverberated between the forsaken ice-coated buildings and which finally reached the ears of the two fleeing figures.

It signalled only one thing to them.

They were coming.

If her heart didn't burst inside her chest in the next two minutes, Martha would be downright astonished. Sweat glued her T-shirt to her back, and advanced in a glistening sheen across her brow. Her muscles screamed for energy but there was little left to give.

She continued to stagger on through the frozen cityscape, supporting the almost deadweight of the old man hanging off her shoulder. She stopped for a moment, heaving him upwards to get a better grip.

'Come on,' she screamed. 'You've got to keep moving!'

The old man looked weakly up at her, his bluish lips parting in what Martha assumed was meant to be a smile. 'I'm sorry,' he croaked, 'I'm so sorry.'

Glancing backwards, through the swirling veils of snow she caught a glimpse of a hunched, misshapen form which darted into a doorway, lost from sight almost immediately. A surge of panic rose in Martha, her mouth dry and acidic. They had to reach the TARDIS, and quickly.

'Stay conscious… you're going into shock… you have to stay awake!' she yelled at the old man. But she was losing him. His body sagged in her arms, his weight dragging her to her knees in the powdery snow. She lay there, her arm protectively thrown over the old man's frail, tissue-thin body. Her mind raced. She had to get up, had to keep going, had to reach the sanctuary of the TARDIS. She had the will, the spirit for fighting. But there was little more she could do as the last vestiges of her energy ebbed into the all-embracing snow. She tried wiggling her fingers. Nothing. Was it frostbite? She'd read about it in textbooks when she was still an everyday medical student. Before her life changed for ever. Back at the Royal Hope Hospital… Royal Hope. That's all she had left – hope…

She desperately tried to focus her mind… Hypothermia, come on, what are the three stages of hypothermia? Stage one, she thought… maybe she should have paid more attention in lectures. What she needed was a doctor. There was irony. Never around when you needed him.

'Doctor,' her voice crackled and broke, as she struggled to stay conscious. 'You said you wouldn't leave me.'

Then, through blurred and stinging eyes, she saw a tall figure stalking towards her, almost lost in the blizzard. That enormous *brown coat billowing, flapping behind him in the wind, his face etched with concern. His eyes seemed to pierce through the snow storm, finding Martha, connecting.*

She felt a swell of warmth rush through her body as adrenalin dumped into her failing system, and she stumbled to her feet, trembling hands outstretched in front of her.

The Doctor stumbled urgently over to her, relief washing across his face. His hands grasped her arms, supporting her, and he grinned.

'Aw, Martha Jones. Where did you get yourself to? Eh? I've been looking for you!'

Martha smiled weakly, wishing she had the energy to think of some pithy and amusing comeback. But then came the exploding red and blossoming black, and somewhere far off the sound of someone falling to the ground.

Then silence.

Four hours earlier by Martha's watch, before the storm swept across the surface of Agelaos, a blue box spun through the iridescent shimmer of the Vortex, buffeted on all sides by the time winds.

Inside the blue box, the impossibly vast organic chamber was suffused with a greenish light that emanated from pulsing circuits rammed higgledy-piggledy under a metal grilled floor. And either side of the jumbled central control console were two figures – Martha Jones and the Doctor.

'So, it's a warning, then?' Martha ventured.

With a flourish of his right hand, the Doctor tipped a switch upwards, snorted, and peered anxiously at the scanner mounted on the console… Glasses now on, he rapped the screen with his knuckles.

'Sounds like a warning to me,' she said.

'Nah!' the Doctor retorted. 'Nothing like a warning!'

An incoherent babble of distorted voices crackled from an ancient speaker grille near the scanner.

The Doctor tugged an ink pen from his inside suit pocket, and began scribbling furiously on a note pad. 'Well, it's not a mayday, and it's not junk mail. Come on, come on, what are you?'

The symbols he scribbled were strange, spidery, and archaic, like alien shorthand.

'Ah!' he exclaimed, straightening up and beaming his best toothy grin, 'Got you!' He hopped backwards onto one of the two pilot's seats at the edge of the console, swinging his long legs back and forth underneath him.

'That's brilliance, that is, Martha Jones. An unknown alien language deciphered in less than, what, ten seconds.' He waved the pad under Martha's nose. 'Oh yes!'

He grinned, and then realised that Martha was staring at him, unimpressed.

'What?' And then his voice notched up a touch: '*What?*'

Martha looked at him. 'It's a warning, isn't it?'

'Yes,' he said, a touch shamefaced.

Martha laughed, and poked him in the ribs, 'What did I tell you? Not just a pretty face, eh?'

The Doctor leaped from the seat, buzzing with pent-up energy. 'I never pay attention to warnings, Martha. Paying attention's for cats! I'm more your golden retriever type, just blunder straight in there all happy and excited! Never got me in to trouble yet… not once in 903 years… well, not quite "not once"… well – sort of all the time really, but you get my point!'

And with that, those long legs powered him round the console, and he was sliding levers, flicking switches.

'Don't you just love this bit?' he enthused. 'Goose pimples, look!' He rolled up the sleeve of his jacket proudly. 'The tingle that goes with the thrill of discovery. We could be anywhere and any when. Isn't that brilliant?'

'Warnings are meant for a reason,' she said levelly.

'That's what I like about you, Martha Jones!'

With a very gentle sideward lurch the TARDIS stopped moving.

The Doctor vaulted the safety rail onto the lower section of the console room floor, and snatched up his fallen brown overcoat. As he tugged the sleeves over his arms, he dashed to the doors.

'Coming?' he said, his hand on the door latch.

'Try and stop me,' and Martha ran down the ramp to join him.

'Are you sure this isn't the Antarctic?' Martha nudged the Doctor gently in the side.

The two of them were standing outside the TARDIS staring at an expanse of ice and snow, as far as the eye could see, rippled and folded into incredible gravity-defying swirls that spread towards the distant curved horizon.

'Not the Antarctic, Martha,' the Doctor stuffed his hands deep into his trouser pockets, and craned his head to peer round the side of the TARDIS.

'Ah!' he said, nodding with dawning realisation. 'Try that way.'

'What?' Martha said, hugging herself against the biting wind.

'Agelaos,' he declared.

Martha carefully poked her head around the edge of the TARDIS. Ahead, in the middle of the ice floe, was a city. Huge bony spires rose thousands of feet into the crisp indigo sky, domes and skyscrapers, bridges and sheer walls of glass, all covered with a dense layer of snow. It looked forgotten, empty, as though it had been swept into a corner and gathered dust.

But most astonishing of all was the sky. Martha was utterly blown away by the beauty of this frozen planet. Above her, shimmering and arcing majestically were aurora borealis; and beyond them shooting stars, flaring, bursting, dissipating; and distant ion cascades, a palette of unimaginably delicate colours suspended in the clear cerulean sky.

And on the distant horizon, hanging just a fraction above the city skyline, burning like a magnesium-white flare was... a sun? No, it was too low, thought Martha, too close to the planet... And, as she peered closer, the white empty space was pulsing, as though breathing. Could black holes be white, she mused? Surely it would destroy everything nearby. So, not a black hole then, but what?

'A wormhole.' The Doctor seemed to guess what she was thinking. 'It's beautiful, isn't it? Your descendants came here to try to harness the energy of that wormhole. A gateway into the Vortex. That's how we got here.'

'But that's mad. Surely it would have, you know…' She struggled to articulate her thoughts.

'Destroyed them? Nah!' The Doctor locked the TARDIS door. 'Fancy a walk?'

'Aggy-what?' she queried, trotting to keep pace with the Doctor's enormous strides.

'Agi-lay-os,' the Doctor pronounced. 'One of the furthest outposts of the Second Great and Bountiful Human Empire. The planet was colonised by a group of 2,000 pioneers from Earth. They terraformed it, or started to.' He scratched his head, ruffling his brown, spiky hair.

'Something happened here?' Martha posed.

'Mm.' He frowned, but forged on regardless.

'What did the warning say?' she persisted. 'Doctor?'

He stopped, swivelled to face her.

'Give or take the odd vowel: "Stay away".'

'From what?'

He started walking again. 'That's the million credit question.'

To Martha it looked like the city had been deserted for years.

At her side the Doctor was chattering on. 'For many centuries they lived on the lip of the wormhole using its energy to power their society. The side effect, though – now, get this, Martha, it's brilliant – the side effect of living so close was that the population began to develop a certain degree of psychic ability.'

Martha raised an eyebrow. 'What? Tea leaves and palm-reading type of psychic?'

'They developed the ability to see strands of future time… that's all being psychic is.' He suddenly stopped dead in his tracks, and Martha virtually cannoned into him.

'What?'

'Shush!' he held his hand up for silence.

'What?' Martha hissed.

The Doctor bought his lips very close to Martha's ear, and whispered, 'When I say run… run.'

Martha felt her skin crawl, and her head suddenly flicked around, her eyes searching the darkened buildings looming over her. She could see nothing, absolutely nothing.

'Run!' yelled the Doctor, grabbing her hand tightly, and yanking her suddenly to the left. Her feet skidding on the snow, she stumbled after him into the shattered shell of a nearby building.

And that's when she heard the weeping…

It was mournful, plaintive at first, but then grew into something more sinister – an animalistic roar that reverberated in Martha's gut. Not the roar of any familiar animal on Earth, nor even any alien she'd ever heard, but something so totally wracked with agony that it chilled her blood. And it was angry.

Worse, it was very close.

The Doctor dragged her through the devastated building, jumping fallen snow-covered girders, pushing aside bundles of cables.

Behind them, they could now hear the panting and snarling of something fast and savage. More scuffling footsteps joined it. They were being hunted by a pack.

As they ascended a fractured set of steps, a creature lurched from the shadows above, only metres ahead of them. Skidding to a halt, the Doctor and Martha turned, ready to hurtle back down the concrete stairs, but found themselves staring, intrigued, at a jumble of creatures below – an illogical mismatch of different species. Insectoid heads, with reptilian arms, or arachnid eyes, or humanoid legs, or gills… the variations were endless. Their lips rode up over cruelly sharp, needle-like teeth, and saliva cascaded in silver torrents across their chins, signalling the intention to kill. And then, hot breath steaming from their open mouths, the creatures all began to wail, a hissing, mournful weeping.

The Doctor clutched Martha's hand tightly, pulling her behind him.

'Cover your eyes! Now!'

From nowhere, what seemed to Martha like a very powerful camera flash went off, searing her eyeballs, leaving her blinking to rid herself of the red flare ghosting in front of her eyes. She clutched her face, burying it in the Doctor's side.

But it was the screaming that truly shocked Martha. The creatures screeched in appalling agony, clutching their heads, reeling drunkenly against the icy walls.

Another brilliant flash.

This time, Martha's vision had cleared enough for her to see the man who stood in the entrance of the shattered building, wrapped in heavy snow gear and wearing thick tinted goggles. In his hand was a snub-nosed black tube that he aimed at the nearest creature. He fired. A flash of bluish light spat from the smoking muzzle. The creature's body twitched rigid, its skin flaring, bubbling like a photograph burning in a flame, then crashed to the ground, utterly senseless.

'Don't just stand there,' the man's voice barked. 'They'll be up in about thirty seconds!'

The Doctor grasped Martha's hand and they raced after him out into the snow. As the wind began to strengthen, it whipped the snow into a whirling frenzy.

'There's a storm coming. We should get inside. My place is that way.' The stranger gestured with a gloved hand.

Martha could just make out a tower in the distance, only thirty metres or so tall, but rising imposingly from the desolation at the centre of the city.

As they drew nearer, Martha spotted a light at the top of the tower, pulsing slowly and regularly, like it was keeping time with a heartbeat. *It's a lighthouse*, she thought, *it's a stupid lighthouse!*

Moments later, they rushed into the base of the tower. The stranger wheeled round and slammed a heavy metal door behind them. Inside it was cool and dark as a cave, but the relief from the wind was welcome. A shaft of light skewered the centre of the room from a tightly curved stairwell, and for a moment that was all that Martha could see. And, then, her eyes began to adjust.

Brushing the snow off his clothes, the man pulled back his hood and tore off his goggles. He was the oldest man Martha had ever seen. His face was gaunt with tissue-thin skin hanging delicately from his cheekbones and the thinnest, whitest hair covering his head. But it was his eyes that shocked Martha: youthful eyes, burning full of passion, deep and beautiful.

The Doctor took the man's spindly hand in both of his, and shook it warmly. 'I don't know who you are but we – Martha and me, that's Martha just there – we are so grateful! Thank you. I'm the Doctor, by the way.'

'Hi!' Martha gave a little wave.

The old man just stared at them, gaping, smiling.

Martha shuffled uncomfortably.

The man finally spoke. 'People? You're actually real?'

'Real as they come, that's me!' the Doctor laughed.

'It's a pleasure. Truly a pleasure. My name is Waechter. Please forgive my manners out there. Those things don't take much notice of decorum. But you'll be safe here.'

The old man turned and began to lead the way up a set of concrete steps.

Martha chased after him. 'We're really grateful, and all that. But, how did you find us?'

'I knew you were coming,' Waechter said, tapping the side of his head. 'I knew where to find you. I'd almost lost hope. I didn't think anybody was coming. Ever again.'

Waechter led the Doctor and Martha up four flights of gloomy stairs to a small, dark room. The room was primitive in the extreme, lit by faintly glowing hexagonal cells strung in a zigzag across the ceiling. A narrow bed occupied one corner of the room. The walls were slick and black with mildew, and the stench was sickening.

Waechter gestured for Martha and the Doctor to sit on the bed.

'What are those creatures?' the Doctor asked after a moment, his eyes darting round the room, taking in every last detail.

'They came through the wormhole,' Waechter said. 'At least, that was the commonly held belief. At the beginning. There's no one left to hold any kind of belief now. Except me. One by one my people vanished. Gone. All of them. Those *things* took them.'

'I'm sorry,' Martha whispered.

Waechter dragged a wooden chair over to the edge of the bed and sat down, his joints creaking. 'You're lucky I knew you were out there,' he continued, 'or they'd have had you too!' He waved the snub-nosed black tube. 'They steer clear of me, by and large.'

'So, what, you're the... last human... on Agelaos?' Martha said.

'Mm,' Waechter nodded. 'I'm the guardian.' He pointed a thin finger skywards. 'I keep the Beacon going.'

The Doctor catapulted off the bed. 'The warning was you?'

Waechter tipped his head, slightly, a thin smile etched across his face.

'But why?'

'It's my job. Maintenance. Chosen by our government. Before they vanished... This beacon was set up to warn people against coming here.'

The Doctor stopped suddenly. 'This beacon's ancient. Surely you haven't been here all that time?'

Waechter looked up at the Doctor, and then pulled down the collar of his sweater to expose his neck. Looking like it had almost grown out of his skin was a small electronic circuit. Tiny wires spread out from the circuit just under the surface of his flesh. A minute green light pulsed softly in the centre of the chip. Waechter tapped the circuit and laughed.

'This stops me from dying. Holds my metabolism in check. I don't get older. I don't get ill. And I don't get to leave. I'm connected to the Beacon. I *can't* leave. And on bad days, this thing really messes around with my psychic ability. Like I said, this is my job. For the rest of time.'

The Doctor put his glasses on and leaned in close to examine Waechter's neck, squinting ever so slightly.

'Aw, it's a beautiful piece of work,' he said. 'Beautiful, but wrong.'

His hand delved into his coat pocket, and he pulled out his psychic paper, flipping it open like an id card. Waechter just stared at the paper, and then turned to the Doctor.

'And?'

'Tell me what you see.'

Waechter leaned in slightly, squinting at the paper. He reached out a spindly hand, taking it from the Doctor. And then Martha jumped as the old man's body tensed, as if he was having a seizure. He cried out, a hollow and haunting moan.

Suddenly he hurled the psychic paper away, and it slid across the dusty floor.

Martha grabbed the Doctor's arm. 'What happened?'

'It's only a guess,' the Doctor said, 'but I think the paper bounced back his own psychic ability. Isn't that brilliant? What did you see?'

Waechter looked at him, his eyes cold. 'My future.'

'We can help, if you want us to?'

Waechter peered into the Doctor's eyes. 'Yes. You could, couldn't you?'

For a moment, the Doctor felt a pang of vulnerability – Waechter had, just for a second, seen into the Time Lord's future, seen everything.

'You know what it's like to live for ever, don't you?' Waechter whispered. 'The passing of eternity with no end in sight. The comings and the goings. And the losses. But on your own it all fades somehow. You hide it away. Once, it was a struggle to forget; now it's a struggle to remember.'

There was a moment of silence.

'You had a family once, Doctor.'

The Doctor struggled with the memory, swallowing hard.

'And now they're lost,' Waechter's eyes misted over. 'Lost to the inferno. In a lake of fire—'

'That's enough,' the Doctor said.

'Can you take me away from here?' Waechter studied the Doctor's face. 'In your... ship. Take me home, to Earth. Get rid of this damn stupid thing in my neck? And just leave me by the sea. It's been frozen here now for almost five centuries. I want to remember what it felt like – the warmth lapping against my skin. Please? Let me die.'

'Where are you going?' Martha asked, as the Doctor leapt to his feet.

'To help him. I'm going to look at this Beacon. Give him his life back.' And then he was gone, bounding up the stairs and out of sight.

Martha gently manoeuvred Waechter over to the bed, and sat him down.

'You're lonely too, aren't you?' Waechter suddenly said. 'I don't have to look inside your mind to know what you want. It's plain for the entire world to see. He's not "the one", for what it's worth.'

Martha smiled gently, but her eyes betrayed the doubt she felt deep inside, 'So you really seriously think you have, what – a gift?'

Waechter laughed, a hoarse, rasping chuckle. 'Oh, I've got a gift, all right. The only problem is, I didn't want it. It wasn't asked for.'

There was a silence between them. And then he spoke, matter-of-fact, out of nowhere.

'Do you want to know how you're going to die?'

'Y… yes, I do.'

'No, you don't.' His eyes penetrated deep into Martha's soul.

'No one can see the future,' she said, a surge of panic rising in her. 'That's just not possible. No way. The future's not happened yet, none of it is written. It just… happens. You're making it up.'

Waechter nodded sagely, looking away from Martha, and down at his hands. He rubbed his thumb across his palm, as if scratching at an annoying itch. 'How could I see the future if it didn't already exist?'

Martha crossed to a tiny window, pondering, and rubbed away the condensation. She pressed her nose against the glass, craning to look down at the blasted cityscape below. Dark, twisted figures were just standing there, sheltered in doorways, staring up at the tower. And they seemed to be weeping.

'What are they doing?' she asked.

Waechter looked round at her, 'Maybe they're lonely too?'

The Doctor bowled back into the room, clapping his hands together. 'Right, then! Allons-y! All done.'

'What's done?' Martha asked.

'A bit of jiggery pokery. Well, more jiggery than pokery. Aaaaanyway! Mr Waechter, how do you fancy going home?'

Waechter's face brightened, his eyes welling with tears.

'I've disconnected the servo relay from the Beacon. You're free.'

Waechter bit his lip, trembling. Martha gently squeezed his shoulder.

'Oh my,' he said, at a loss for all other expression.

Martha picked up the weapon off the bed, and handed it to the Doctor. 'There's a crowd of those things outside. You go first. Distract them with this. I'll bring Waechter once the coast is clear. Meet you at the TARDIS.'

He took the tube from her, perplexed. 'Will it hurt them?'

Waechter smiled. 'Not as much as I'd like it to. Vicious brutes. It'll sting, though. Nasty headache. No more.'

'Marvellous!' The Doctor headed for the door, stopped, and spun round on his heels, his sneakers squeaking on the floor.

'Coming?'

Seconds later, he bounded out into the storm. As he disappeared into the swirling gloom pursued by the shuffling creatures, Martha, with a gradually weakening Waechter at her side, stepped out into the snow.

Martha was somewhere in the dark. There was a break in her memory. She remembered the Doctor stalking towards her through the storm, talking to her, and then nothing. On the other side of the break, she was looking up at the Doctor as he lifted her from her fallen position in the snow. And for now she was content to drift in and out of consciousness, knowing that she was completely safe. Even when she seemed to recall the creatures attacking, and blinding flashes of light bursting from the Doctor's hand, she didn't feel threatened.

But gradually everything became clear and sharp. The Doctor had managed to drag her and Waechter steadily towards the TARDIS. Finally the rectangular blue shape emerged from the slashing snow. With a last desperate push, stumbling to her feet, Martha reached out, gratefully caressing the wooden sides of the police box. The Doctor took one final look behind him at the desolate ice floe. A series of dark, shuffling shapes emerged from the storm in the distance, their bodies crusted with ice. He tossed Waechter's weapon over his shoulder and stepped into the ship.

Inside at last, Martha helped Waechter up the ramp to the central console, guiding him to the two pilot's seats.

The old man's head swung wildly around, taking in every detail of the cavernous expanse – the coral-like columns that seemed to grow out of the floor, and push up high into the domed ceiling; the rusted railings wrapped in padding, secured with duct tape. 'This is… is… unbelievable,' he stuttered.

'You'll get used to it,' Martha said, as she sat him down.

The Doctor stalked up to the console, throwing off his overcoat.

'Last chance to say no,' he said.

Waechter took a deep breath, and grasped Martha's hand.

'What are you saying damn fool things like that for?' he said. 'You sound like you want me to change my mind.'

The Doctor laughed, and flipped a switch upwards with an expansive gesture.

Within seconds, the grinding and wheezing sound of the TARDIS engines filled the console room, and Waechter stared in wonder at the rising and falling of the central column.

'This machine is incredible—' he began, and then broke off as he clutched at the circuit in his neck and let out a wail of terrible pain. He crumpled to the floor, crackles of green electricity dancing and sparking around his neck and face.

'He can't die here,' Martha shouted. 'It shouldn't happen here and now, like this!'

'We've got to go back,' the Doctor raced to the console, slamming levers down frantically.

The TARDIS juddered and shook, and within seconds the central column stopped moving as the craft landed once more.

'I thought you'd disconnected him?' asked Martha.

The Doctor raced over to Waechter, plucking out the sonic screwdriver. He waved it across the chip in the old man's neck, and then examined the readings.

'Oh, I'm so stupid!' He smacked his forehead with the flat of his hand. 'It's a two-way mechanism. If the Beacon fails to hold him here, then the chip kicks in as a back-up. That's so elementary. Why didn't I *think* of that?'

Martha drew the Doctor to one side. 'Can't you just turn it off?'

The Doctor frowned, his face a mask of concentration. 'It's not that simple. That thing is hard-wired into his biology. I might kill him. No, I've got to be clever about this.'

Spinning on his heels, the Doctor tore over to the console, and his hands began flashing across the dials and levers, occasionally scanning something with his sonic screwdriver.

Martha sat down next to Waechter, holding one of his fragile, bony hands in hers. 'Trust him,' she said.

Waechter looked at her. 'I'm stuck here, aren't I?'

Martha shook her head. 'He'll find a way.'

The Doctor suddenly leapt away from the console and ran to Waechter's side, waving the sonic screwdriver.

'You're in the company of a genius, did you know that?' He beamed. 'I can jam your circuit's link to the Beacon, and once it's jammed I can deactivate it.'

Waechter looked at Martha, seemingly for reassurance, and then back at the Doctor. 'And then you can take me home?'

'Oh, yes!' The Doctor leaned in close to Waechter's neck. 'This might sting a touch,' he warned.

Martha knew immediately that 'sting a touch' meant it would hurt like crazy, so she gripped the old man's hand tightly.

The buzzing blue tip of the sonic screwdriver hovered over the centre of the chip, and the surface electronics began to shimmer and vibrate. Waechter screwed his eyes up as he began to feel waves of heat pulsate out from his neck. Suddenly a shower of sparks erupted from his neck, but the Doctor kept on working, his tongue poking between his lips.

As Martha held Waechter's hand she began to feel it swelling in her grip, and she looked down. As she unfurled her fingers she realised in horror that she was holding not an old man's hand, but something that resembled a claw bristling with tough, spiny hairs. She dropped it and backed away.

'Doctor,' she whispered.

The Doctor looked over, following the direction of her gaze. 'Oh,' he said. 'Now that's not fair!'

Waechter, his face still contorted with pain, looked at his hand. 'What's happening to me?'

His face grim, the Doctor's shoulders sagged with realisation. 'Of course! It's a new brain I need, Martha. This one's getting tired! I know what's happening!'

Martha looked up at him, confused.

'Don't you see?' He was bursting with energy. 'Oh, lazy, lazy brain, Doctor! I know what this is all about.'

Martha, frustrated, snapped, 'What?'

'It's the curse of this planet.' The Doctor straightened up. 'You were wrong, Waechter. The inhabitants haven't gone anywhere, they've not been murdered. They're still here. They've *evolved* into these alien creatures.'

Martha looked on in horror as Waechter's arm began to twist and elongate, transforming into something horribly similar to a spider's leg.

The Doctor, fascinated, popped his glasses on. 'It's got to be the influence of the wormhole. Not only has it given the inhabitants incredible psychic powers, it's also irradiated their bodies with who knows how many thousands of types of alien DNA that have passed through the Vortex.'

Waechter cried out in agony, his right arm cracking and splintering as it doubled in length. 'Please, help me!'

'It's the chip,' the Doctor said. 'His humanity was being held in check by the chip. That was what was stopping him from turning into one of those things. There's got to be *something* I can do!' He turned on the sonic screwdriver again, and the circuit rippled and spat sparks. 'I can do this!'

Waechter screamed once more, his face contorting in agony. His jaw suddenly began to mutate, distorting into two separate mandibles.

'I am not one of those *things!*' Waechter spat.

'You're making it worse!' Martha shouted.

The Doctor turned off the screwdriver. 'No! No! No!! Why can't I do this?'

The old man's tongue poked between his lips, now blackened and swollen. It flickered in and out, like a snake scenting the air.

The Doctor took a deep breath, and ran the palms of his hands over his strained face.

'Doctor?' Martha said urgently.

'OK!' he snapped, and knelt down in front of Waechter. 'Listen to me. If I destroy that chip, you will turn into one of these creatures. But if I repair it to keep you human, then I can't take you away from here. I'm sorry. One way or the other, you're going to have to stay. There's nothing else I can do. I really am so sorry. You have to tell me what you want me to do. Waechter?'

The old man brandished his claw-like protuberance, staring in utter horror at it.

'Is this all that my life has been about?' he cried. 'Just waiting for *this*?'

The Doctor continued urgently: 'Please! What do you want me to do?'

And as Waechter struggled to make his decision, and the Doctor and Martha waited with bated breath, the sound of weeping could be heard… from outside on the snow-blasted wastes. The creatures – *his people* – were waiting, too.

Waechter reached out a twisted claw and rested it gently on the Doctor's shoulder. 'Your identification paper…'

'The psychic paper?'

'Yes. May I see it again? Please?'

The Doctor reached into his jacket, and pulled out the wallet. He slowly opened it, showing it to Waechter. The old man stared deep into its intuitive heart and his reaction this time was sedate, almost serene.

'Thank you,' he said softly.

The Doctor closed the wallet and tucked it away. 'What did you see?'

Waechter leant back in the chair, and closed his eyes. 'An end. And a beginning. Running free. Never lonely again.' He opened his eyes, and smiled. 'I owe you my thanks.'

The Doctor waved his hand in front of his face. 'Nonsense.'

'It's our custom here, Doctor. I owe you a gift. And the only gift I have of value is my knowledge of the future.'

The Doctor stood up, frowning, and backed away slightly. 'I'm not sure it's wise to know what's coming. More fun that way.'

Ignoring him, Waechter turned to Martha. 'Look to your family. Protect them. They will need you to be strong, so very strong, Martha Jones.'

Martha's face clouded with confusion. 'What do you mean?'

Waechter looked up at the Doctor. 'And for you, Time Lord, there are endings coming. There will be loss and death—'

'Please,' the Doctor broke in. 'Don't.'

Waechter looked down at his hooked, clawed hands. His breathing shallow and rasping. When he looked up again, his eyes were shot green, pulsing with inner light. 'Please destroy this thing in my neck,' he said, his voice barely a whisper. 'Let me go. I want to be with my people.'

The Doctor leant forward, activating the sonic screwdriver, disabling the circuit. An incandescent shower of sparks erupted from the old man's neck, and his back suddenly arched, his face contorted in a rictus of pain.

New bolts of agonising pain wracked his body.

He gasped for air.

He fell to his knees and then forward on his hands. As his bone and muscle bent and reformed themselves, his face began to distort, bulging, puckering and swelling into some new creature.

Martha turned away, and the Doctor watched her cross to the console.

'Martha?' he asked.

'I don't want to see,' she told him.

Behind her, the Doctor gently helped the creature to its feet. It swung its head round to look at the Doctor, its bulbous, arachnid eyes peering quizzically at him. And then, the creature bowed its head, respectfully.

'I'll help you outside,' the Doctor murmured. He pushed the doors open, and freezing air billowed into the console room.

Martha stood utterly still at the console, listening to the click-clack of Waechter's new feet on the metal TARDIS floor, her face streaked with tears.

Martha could hear that Waechter had paused by the door, but still she couldn't bring herself to turn around. Was he waiting for some sign, some gesture from her? Feeling guilty and selfish, she sighed, and turned slowly to face him, dreading what she might see.

But he had already gone, stepped out into the snow.

The Doctor solemnly closed the door, and sauntered back up towards Martha. He put his arm around her shoulders, and pulled her close for a moment.

'I love a happy ending,' he said.

Martha looked up at him. 'What now?' she said.

'Oh, you know. A bit more jiggery pokery,' he beamed. 'You know, Martha Jones, I think that Beacon should start transmitting a very different message.'

'Like what?'

'Something more appropriate. What do you say, eh? How about… *a protected planet of special scientific interest*,' he ventured.

As the Doctor began to set the coordinates on the console for the Beacon, and the central column began to rise and fall, Martha asked, 'He will be all right, won't he?'

The Doctor stared at the console's pulsing lights, and for a moment he looked surprisingly optimistic.

'Maybe, maybe not,' he said. 'But, there's one thing he will be, Martha.'

'Oh yeah? What's that?' she asked.

The Doctor twisted a button on the console. 'Brilliant!'

FOUR

Martha's story seemed to raise the little girl's spirits. Just telling it had done Martha the power of good. It had forcibly reminded her of the things that really mattered. Here was a little girl, nine years old, who'd survived for two weeks on the simple hope that someone was going to make everything better. It made Martha ashamed for feeling put upon and sorry for herself.

Martha took a shower in the flat's dank cubicle. The water was cold, and intermittent, but she hardly cared. She washed the traces of perfume off her and vowed not to wear any again, and no jewellery, either.

It was nearly dawn. Aleesha was asleep. They had eaten a meal – beans and sausages out of a tin, cooked on a camp stove Martha carried in her rucksack. Martha tied her hair back. She found a pair of trainers in the bedroom that were a reasonable fit.

When Aleesha woke up, Martha would take her to somewhere safer. She'd find a survivor collective or a refugee group, and make sure they took care of the little girl. Martha felt a renewed determination. She'd wasted too much time hiding and skulking around, questioning her own abilities. She had a job to do, an enormous job, and she just had to get on with it. No more hiding, no more living in the shadows. She had to be positive and confident. She had to move with a purpose and make her own luck.

That's what he'd do, after all.

Daybreak. Griffin stood beside the Humvee, sipping hot coffee from a tin mug. Rafferty and the other team members had groused about the fruitless night's search, but Griffin wasn't convinced it had been fruitless.

He was sure they'd been very close. Though she was clever and disguised, the elusive Martha Jones had been almost in their grasp. It was a gut feeling, and Griffin knew to trust his gut feelings. Just blind luck, or the mischance of a famished dog breaking a window pane, had allowed her to slip away this time. But if he could get this close once, he could do it again.

Griffin tipped the dregs of the coffee out onto the ground and called to his men. He wasn't going to give up and let her get away. The ADC had been smart to pick him for the job. Griffin was like a cruise missile. Once you set him going, he didn't stop until he found the target.

'Come on!' he shouted. 'Let's go!'

Martha said goodbye to Aleesha two days later at a survivor outpost in Battersea. Martha spent a few hours with the group, talking to them, listening to their stories and telling some of her own. She made them listen, she made them understand, and she made them promise to carry the word on to any other groups they ran across.

'Why are you doing this?' one of the survivors asked her.

'Because someone has to,' Martha replied. 'Just tell them. Just tell them what Martha Jones told you.'

'He'll come looking for you,' said one of the others. 'You go around telling people this stuff, telling people your name, the Master will come looking for you.'

'I know,' said Martha. 'He already is. But look at it this way. If the Master himself wants to stop me, what I'm saying must be pretty important.'

When she went to find Aleesha to say goodbye, Martha found her earnestly telling the story Martha had told her to a group of refugee children. Not wanting to interrupt, Martha watched quietly and waited until Aleesha had finished.

The process was beginning.

She gave Aleesha a hug. 'These people will look after you,' she said.

'Do you want your earrings back?' Aleesha asked.

'You keep them for me. I'm coming back.'

Aleesha nodded. 'OK, but you had better have something in return,' Aleesha said. 'Here.'

She held something out to Martha. It was a plastic badge that read, 'Hooray! I am Nine!'

'I'll treasure it,' said Martha.

She picked up her backpack.

'Aleesha?'

'Yes, Martha?'

'Thank you.'

'What for?'

Martha smiled. 'It doesn't matter. Just thank you.'

She turned, and headed towards the gate. It was starting to rain.

'Martha?' Aleesha called after her. 'Martha, where are you going?'

'Everywhere,' said Martha.

FIVE

At night, the ruins of Lille glowed like a pale ghost. There were deep fires in the rubble of the sundered town, fires that had been burning for seven weeks, since the descent of the Toclafane on Day Zero.

Directed by Over Watch, UCFA Brunol led his reaction force through the enclaves of the labour camps, and onto a broken highway that ran into the industrial wasteland of Surcourt. They gave the radiation pits a wide berth and kept clear of the razor-wire barricades.

To the north, beyond Surcourt, the spectre of Lille underlit the night sky.

The trucks and APCs in his small convoy rolled to a halt. Over Watch, the command-and-control data network that fed through the Archangel satellite grid and coordinated UCF operations, had been routing them into Surcourt, where a suspected flash market was under way.

Now the command was to stop and wait.

Brunol, eager to get on, requested clarification. As

he waited, he drummed his fingers impatiently on the dashboard. Tap-tap-tap-tap! Tap-tap-tap-tap!

The network pinged.

<Hold position and await personnel rendezvous> the message window from Over Watch read.

After five minutes, a small truck approached from the south and pulled up beside the convoy. The men who got out were armed, but they weren't wearing UCF uniforms. They were a scrappy lot dressed in dirty fatigues and worn-out army surplus kit.

Brunol didn't like the look of them. He checked his sidearm and got out of his APC to meet them.

'What's this about?' he asked.

The leader of the newcomers was a big fellow with a scarred face.

'You had your instructions to wait?' the man asked Brunol in French, but his accent sounded British.

'Yes. Identify yourself.'

The man flashed an ID wallet. 'UCFA Griffin. Special operations.'

'Why aren't you in uniform?' Brunol asked.

'Special operations,' Griffin repeated.

'This is a waste of time,' said Brunol. He gestured down the road towards Surcourt. 'There's a flash market in progress. They picked off a supply convoy yesterday, and they're dispersing the goods. We should be in there, breaking it up and making arrests, not—'

'Have you seen this woman?' Griffin asked, holding up a photo.

'No. Should I have?'

'You've heard of her, though,' said Griffin. 'Her name's Martha Jones.'

Brunol raised his eyebrows. 'Martha Jones? I've heard stories. She's some kind of figurehead, isn't she?' he asked.

'I've been tracking her across the UK. She slipped into France eight days ago, on a container ship, and went through two internment camps on the coast. I have positive sightings. She looped down through Cambrai, but I think she's turned back to cross the border into Belgium.'

'What am I supposed to do about it?' asked Brunol.

'Hold your forces back until I signal you.'

'Why?'

'Because a flash market is exactly the sort of place she'd go. She's contacting survivor groups. I need that market to stay open a while longer. You close it down, you close down my lead.'

Brunol shrugged. 'Is this authorised?'

'Yes,' said Griffin. He held up a phone. 'But if you don't believe me, there's someone you can talk to.'

They'd chosen an old warehouse to hold the market in. It was near the container yard in the south of Surcourt with good access, in and out, and hard to contain or close off.

Speed was the essence of a flash market. You put the word out, and then moved in and set up fast, distributing goods from the backs of lorries. First come, first served. Get the goods into circulation, and then everybody fades into the night, as fast as they'd come, and no one knew the market had ever been there.

It worked in principle. Mathieu Vivier knew plenty of

flash markets that had been hit by the UCF. In Saint-Omer, just the week before, twenty people had been gunned down at a flash market in a sports centre.

The risk was worth it, though. It was the only way to get food and medicines and other vital supplies moving into the survivor networks. Nowhere was secure enough to store the quantities of goods taken from a convoy hijack. You had to get it broken down and into circulation. In the post-Day Zero world, survival depended on speed, mobility and minimising your exposure.

The market was busy. There were people in from all over the countryside. By the light of oil-drum fires, they sorted through the loads – tonight, mostly clothing and tinned goods – in the trucks and barrows.

Mathieu was watching the doors. He had a sports air horn in his coat pocket. They had men posted outside, and lookouts on the rooftops and approach roads. The first sign of a UCF raid or descending Toclafane, they would shut up shop and scatter.

Mathieu moved through the crowd, greeting faces he knew, nodding to others. A lot of newcomers had turned up, and that made him edgy.

'Looking for something in particular?' he asked one of the strangers.

'The usual,' the man replied. 'Food.'

'English, right?' asked Mathieu.

The man laughed. 'My accent that bad, eh?'

'Little way from home, aren't you?' Mathieu asked him.

'I was over here on holiday when it went down,' the man said. 'Guess I'm stuck here. Come to that, I don't think anywhere is home any more, do you?'

Mathieu shook his head.

'Actually,' said the man, 'I'm looking for someone too.'

'Yeah?'

The man took a scuffed photo out of his coat. 'My girlfriend. She was on holiday with me. We got separated. I really want to find her.'

'What's her name?' Mathieu asked, looking at the photo.

'Martha,' the man said. 'I just want to find her. I'm so worried about her.'

'I wish I could help you,' said Mathieu, 'but I don't recognise her. And I'd remember a face like that.'

'Thanks, anyway.'

'I'll ask around,' Mathieu said. 'Maybe someone will know.'

The man moved away. Mathieu watched him for a moment, then moved on. He stopped to warm his hands at one of the oil-drum fires.

'Funny bloke,' said a voice beside him quietly.

Mathieu looked around, but there didn't seem to be anyone there.

Except there was. A girl was standing beside him, just at the edge of his peripheral vision.

'Don't look at me, look at him,' she said. 'Pretty well fed, don't you think? Pretty well fed, for one of us.'

Mathieu stared through the bustling crowd. He could still see the English stranger. He'd stopped to show the crumpled photo to someone else. He was a big guy. He didn't look hungry.

'What are you telling me?' Mathieu said.

'I'm telling you that the UCF have all the rations they need. I'm telling you this market has to close now because we're in real danger.'

Mathieu turned to look at her. Even facing her, he couldn't quite see her, but he could see enough to know that it was the girl from the photograph.

'What's your name?' she asked.

'Mathieu.'

'You have to trust me, Mathieu,' she said. 'You have to trust me, or people are going to die.'

Mathieu looked back at the English stranger. He had turned, and was staring directly at Mathieu. A slight grin crossed his mouth and curled the big scar on his cheek.

'My name's Martha,' the girl said. 'You have to trust me.'

Griffin turned. The guy he'd quizzed was standing beside an oil drum, staring straight at him. The flickering oil-drum fire was casting the man's shadow out behind him in the gloom. But the shadow wasn't flickering.

It wasn't a shadow. He could see her. Right there in the amber dark. *He could see her.*

He began to move, pushing through the crowd, shoving people aside. He reached under his coat for his Glock.

But the man beside the oil drum had pulled out an air horn and was letting it blast.

Pandemonium swept through the marketplace. Other air horns started to blare, taking up the alarm. People were shouting, scrambling, and surging towards the exits. Engines were starting up, trucks thundering into life. Exhaust fumes belched. Panic took hold.

'Out of my way!' Griffin yelled, fighting his way through the stampeding crowd. He couldn't get through. He got a glimpse of her. She was running with the guy with the air horn.

Griffin raised his Glock and fired two shots at the roof. The spent cases pinged as they hit the ground. The crowd around him scattered in terror, spilling away to get as far from him as possible. He started to run again, but a flatbed truck reversed right out in front of him and nearly knocked him down.

He ran around it, cursing, colliding with people running the other way. He'd lost sight of her. Where was she?

From outside, bursts of gunfire began to chatter. The panic went up a gear. People were screaming. An oil drum went over in a swirl of sparks and cinders. Two pick-ups collided as they tried to drive for the same door.

Still running, Griffin pulled out his radio. 'Close in! Secure the zone! She's here! Repeat, she's here!'

SIX

Martha and Mathieu ran headlong with the crowd. There was gunfire outside. It sounded as if a whole army was storming the warehouse.

'Have you got transport?' she yelled at him.

'Yes, yes! Come on!'

When a raid hit a market, you just got yourself out. Every man for himself, that was the rule. Get out, vanish. Worry about the others later. If you stopped to help someone, you weren't helping yourself.

But this girl – Martha – had probably saved lives with her warning. A lot of lives. She'd pre-empted the raid. She'd got them all moving before the UCF was in position.

So he wasn't going to leave her.

Mathieu had an old Citroën van parked near the west door of the warehouse. They ran to it, and Mathieu jumped in and started the engine as Martha climbed in on the passenger side.

'We've got to move!' Martha cried.

'I know! I know!' Mathieu replied, fighting to find first gear.

Martha heard a series of dull thumps, like the sound of someone flicking stiff cardboard with their fingers. She realised that bullets were thumping into the van's rear bodywork. She glanced in her door mirror and saw the big UCF agent with the scarred face sprinting up behind them. He was firing his pistol. Martha yelped and flinched as the sidelights of her window shattered. A bullet creased the dashboard.

Mathieu lurched the van forward, his foot down. Blue smoke boiled from the tyres. They hurtled towards the west door, knocking over stacked cartons of tinned fruit. In her door mirror, Martha could see their pursuer. He was fit and powerful, and the length of his stride was keeping him close behind the van as it accelerated. He fired his Glock again, the rounds punching into the van's rear doors.

'He's right behind us!' Martha yelled.

'I know,' said Mathieu. 'Hold on.'

The old van's rear lights had long since been smashed. When Mathieu hit the brakes, there were no red lights to warn of the sudden stop.

At full stretch, Griffin suddenly realised that the van had slammed to a halt. He collided with the rear doors at full tilt and bounced off them onto the ground, dazed.

Mathieu threw the van forwards again, and accelerated out of the west door into the night.

Behind them, Griffin picked himself up and reached for his radio.

***

Trucks and cars were fleeing the warehouse in all directions. They drove fast, without lights, risk balancing risk.

Not everyone would make it. The UCF reaction force had swept in and already blocked some of the routes south. Heavy gunfire rattled and flashed in the night.

Mathieu wrenched on the steering wheel to avoid a slower-moving market truck, then left the road completely. Martha clung on. They jolted across an old playing field and out through a gate onto a service road that ran between derelict factory units and a patch of waste ground.

'Look out!' Martha cried.

A UCF truck had swung out at them, headlights blazing. There was gunfire. Mathieu tried to turn, but a tyre blew out and the van went into a skid. It tore through a chain-link fence, left the ground briefly, and then rolled and bounced down an embankment onto the waste ground.

'Any sign?' asked Griffin.

Rafferty scrambled up the embankment from the wrecked van. The area was bathed in floodlights from UCF vehicles.

'Nothing,' said Rafferty. 'Though there's some blood in the cab. Someone's hurt.'

'They can't have gone far,' said Griffin.

He turned to UCFA Brunol. 'Close this entire zone down. Full deployment. Lock everything down. We've got two hours before dawn. She's not getting away this time.'

'Hold still,' said Martha.

'Leave it,' Mathieu replied.

'You've got chips of windscreen glass in your face,' she said, 'so hold still.'

'We've got people who can do this,' said one of the women watching them. Her name was Sylvie.

'I'm a doctor,' said Martha.

The survivor camp Mathieu had brought her to was about five miles west of Surcourt. They'd reached it at first light. It was a ruined factory, with no sign of life or habitation, but ingeniously concealed doors led down into an extensive basement level where over fifty people lived.

They had a water supply, provisions, a serviceable latrine, and they'd even built a ducting system to channel cooking smoke out without giving away their location.

'More than one of us had grandparents in the Resistance,' Mathieu said. 'Stories get handed down. Stories. Ideas. Techniques.'

'I've got some stories of my own,' said Martha.

'Maybe you start with the obvious one,' said a man called Yves. 'Who are you?'

'She's a wanted person,' said a woman called Lisel. 'The UCF are after her. Mathieu shouldn't have brought her here.'

'I couldn't leave her outside,' said Mathieu, wincing slightly as Martha's tweezers removed another lump of glass from his cheek. 'Besides, her warning saved lives. It would have been a slaughter.'

'It's bad enough,' said Yves. 'There are dozens dead, dozens more arrested. The whole zone is locked down. Patrols everywhere. We'll have to stay underground for weeks. No foraging. No resupply. Food will go short.'

'That's if they don't find us anyway,' said Lisel.

Martha could hear the despair in their voices. She could see the hollow looks on their faces, the fear in their eyes, especially the younger ones, and the children.

They made her think of Aleesha.

'Listen,' she said, 'listen to me…'

Breathing Space

Martha felt a thrill of anticipation whenever she stepped from the TARDIS. With the Doctor anything was possible. Their last stop had been the holiday planet of Nacre, where the beaches had seemed endless and twin suns had warmed the clear blue water. It had been fantastic.

But not, she thought, gazing down, anything like as fantastic as Earth.

The Doctor said something and, although he was standing right next to her, Martha barely heard a word. It was impossible to drag her eyes away from the globe that shone through the oblong display window stretching right the way around the curved room. For all the wonders she had seen during her travels, there really was no place like home.

'I *said*,' a voice murmured into her ear, 'are you going to stand there gawping all day? We're not on holiday any more, you know.'

Martha sighed, remembering the tranquillity of Nacre. Not to mention the attentions of the hotel's extremely handsome waiters. Pity the Doctor couldn't sit still for more than five minutes or she'd still have been there.

'And there was me thinking you knew how to show a girl a good time.'

'This *is* a good time.' The Doctor's reflection grinned at her in the glass. 'Come on, who wants to laze around on a beach when there's a mystery to solve? Those transmissions the TARDIS intercepted. The whale song – ring any bells?'

Reality came crashing back, and Martha remembered where they were. On a space station; a big one, if the endless but eerily deserted corridors were anything to go by. The large, round room they were in reminded her of those old images of NASA mission control. Curved rows of workstations radiated from a central hub, each occupied by a man or woman peering into monitors.

Martha half-expected to see guards approaching. But she and the Doctor might have been invisible for all the attention anyone paid them.

If only she knew why the TARDIS had brought them here, materialising in a storage hangar in the depths of the station. It obviously had something to do with those strange signals, which had sounded to her like whale song. Maybe they came from the giant spacecraft she could see. There were hundreds of them, drifting across the planet so slowly they hardly seemed to be moving.

'Those ships, are they human or alien?'

'You lot don't have ships that big in 2088.' The Doctor squinted at them. 'Anyway, they're not ships.'

'Then what are they?'

'No idea.'

'I thought you knew everything.' Martha peered out again and recoiled as a metallic sphere bristling with antennae rushed through space towards her. She took an involuntary step back, expecting it to smash through the glass, sighing with relief when it veered away at the last moment and disappeared. 'What was that?'

'Oh, just one of the monitor probes.'

Martha jumped. It wasn't the Doctor who'd answered. She spun round.

A kindly-looking elderly man with thick glasses and receding hair smiled at her. The smile faltered slightly. 'Sorry, I don't think we've met. I take it you're one of the new arrivals. I'm Conrad Morris—'

'Professor Morris!' The Doctor grabbed the man's arm. 'I'm such an admirer of your work. Martha, this is the genius who rewrote the rulebook on bioengineering. Then tore it up and wrote a completely *new* rulebook!'

'Oh, nonsense!' Morris protested, but he looked rather pleased.

'John Smith,' the Doctor said, flashing his psychic paper. 'This is my associate Doctor Martha Jones. Sorry we're late, couldn't resist the duty free shop.'

Morris barely had time to acknowledge Martha before the Doctor was steering him away from the window. 'Now where was I? Oh yes! Those huge things in the sky, the signals – don't really have to say much more, do I?'

'Indeed not. There's still a lot of data to analyse, as you can imagine, but the provisional results are extremely promising. In fact, far better than we could possibly have imagined – it seems the Benefactors were not exaggerating.'

Martha was lost. 'What's going on here? And who are the Benefactors?'

'Have you been underground for the last month?' Morris asked, not unkindly.

'Actually, yeah, she has,' the Doctor said, 'deep underground, testing this new theory about stalactites. Or was it stalagmites? Which are the ones that grow down? Anyway, never mind! You were going to tell Martha about the Benefactors.'

The professor carried on walking, the Doctor at his side. Martha fell in beside them, determined not to be left behind.

'The Benefactors, it appears, are the salvation of mankind,' Morris said, rather pompously. 'It sounded too good to be true, at first, and there was no shortage of sceptics. But, judging by the initial results, the sceptics were wrong.'

Martha shook her head, still baffled. 'Why don't you start at the beginning? I've been... away, don't forget.'

'I'd like to know who these Benefactors are,' the Doctor said. 'I mean, don't you think it's a bit of a coincidence, being the good guys and having a name like the *Benefactors*? It'd be like having bad guys called the Villains.'

Morris shrugged. 'It was probably just a literal translation.'

'So, those big floating things,' Martha said. 'They're the Benefactors, right?'

'Hardly. The Benefactors remain many thousands of light years away. They are a solitary race. What you see is the gift they sent us.'

'I still don't get it.'

'Wait until we reach central analysis,' the professor told her. 'I'll replay the broadcast for you both. Then everything will become clear.'

'Broadcast, eh?' The Doctor grinned. 'Good! I haven't seen any TV in ages.'

Morris led them along an aisle that ran between the banks of monitors until they reached the central hub, a large oval desk laden with equipment. Standing around it, gazing up at screens suspended overhead, were a dozen or so people, all dressed in white coats. Martha guessed they must be the more important scientists on board.

The screens streamed lines of data that meant nothing to her but obviously spoke volumes to the scientists, scribbling away with styli on hand-held pads as they studied them. One broke off to confer quietly with a keyboard operator. Otherwise no one said a word. There were no friendly conversations, no laughter and no coffee breaks. There was a definite tension in the air.

'Not much office banter is there?' she said lightly.

Morris frowned. 'Not when the future of the world is at stake, Doctor Jones. Everyone here has family and friends on Earth. People they care about.'

'Sorry, I didn't mean…'

'No, no, I'm sure you didn't,' the professor said, smiling to show he was not offended. 'But you must understand, we are in the front line. We'll be the first to know if the

Benefactors were right or, God forbid, if they were wrong and the Earth is doomed. That's a heavy burden.'

'Funny thing,' the Doctor said. 'I have no idea who these Benefactors are or what they're doing, but I've already taken a dislike to them. Save the planet or don't save it, but don't keep people dangling. I hate dangling.'

A serious-looking man who had been standing at the side of the hub now approached them. He wore a dark suit and fiddled with his flashy wristwatch.

'Hello!' the Doctor said brightly. 'Who're you, then?'

'Daniel Grant,' the man answered, face a granite mask. 'Head of security.'

The Doctor flashed his psychic paper again and introduced them both.

'I should have guessed your people would send someone here,' Grant sneered. His eyes swept over the Doctor, taking in his shock of hair and the pinstripe suit that clashed with his trainers. 'You don't look like a scientist.'

'Doctor Smith's a bit eccentric but a genius,' Martha said.

'Right on both counts,' the Doctor beamed. 'Now, then, I believe Professor Morris was going to replay the Benefactors' broadcast for us.'

'Why?' Grant was openly suspicious. 'Is there anyone on Earth who hasn't seen it a hundred times already?'

'Let's make it a hundred and one,' the Doctor said, putting on his glasses and peering expectantly at the screens. 'Never know, could have missed something.'

Grant stared at him. 'Fine, whatever, but I think you're just wasting time.'

Professor Morris stepped across to the nearest workstation and spoke quietly to the operator. 'Won't be a moment,' he said as he rejoined them. 'You know, I'll never forget the first time I saw it. I was filled with such *hope*.'

'Why?' Martha asked.

'Because the world was dying, that's why! Atmospheric pollution, global warming, it was all reaching critical point. The world's governments played it down. They didn't want mass panic on their hands. But the evidence was there for everyone to see – the icecaps melting, the floods, the air so choked with noxious gases that some days it hurt to breathe.'

Martha could scarcely believe it. Everyone had been talking about global warming for as long as she could remember, but she hadn't thought too much about it. It was something to worry about in the future. Now, it seemed, was that time.

'So when the Benefactors made contact,' the professor continued, eyes far away, 'it was like our prayers had been answered. But of course you know all that.'

'*Course* we do,' the Doctor said. 'But I can never resist a good story. Go on – what happened next?'

A burst of static interrupted the data stream on the screen immediately overhead. As soon as Martha saw the creature that appeared on it she was shocked into numbness. '*People of Earth,*' it said. Its voice sounded composed of liquid, like someone gargling while they talked. '*We feel your planet's suffering. We feel your pain and your terror. But do not be afraid. We can help you.*'

Martha barely took in the words; she was too transfixed

by the alien speaking them. Its impossibly long head was like a living balloon, with tiny eyes near the top and a slit of a mouth at the other end. It was the colour of dough and did not appear to have ears or a nose. The head quivered as it spoke, as though under-filled with gas. If that was its head, Martha thought with a shudder, she was glad she couldn't see its body.

'No,' she heard, a breathy gasp that for a moment she thought was coming from the speakers. Then she realised it was the Doctor, not the alien, that had spoken. The smile had vanished from his face and he was staring at the bizarre creature with an expression somewhere between anger and loathing.

'We have the technology to scour your atmosphere, to remove the poisonous gases and give your planet the chance to breathe again.'

'No!' the Doctor repeated, so loudly that everyone turned to stare at him. 'You have to stop them. If you don't, everyone will die.'

'What are you talking about?' Morris demanded.

'For this we seek nothing in return.'

'Don't believe a word that thing's saying.' The Doctor waved a finger at the screen. 'I've seen those creatures before. Believe me, they are *not* beneficial.'

Grant sneered. 'They make contact for the first time and you've seen them before. Very good, Doctor – I suppose you speak their language, too.'

'Their language is destruction,' the Doctor said, fixing Grant with an intense look which reminded Martha that beneath the slightly geeky human façade was an alien who had seen far more than a mere human could imagine.

'They're the Cineraria. They take planets by stealth, wipe out all life and then strip out every resource until there's nothing left but ashes and the stink of death.'

Grant smiled coldly. 'You call it stealth when they contact us, offer help and send life forms far beyond our understanding? Life forms which can filter the atmosphere, collecting greenhouse gases that will be discharged into space? If they wanted to take Earth, *Doctor*, why not just attack it? They're so advanced we wouldn't stand a chance.'

'That's not how they work. The Cineraria don't go for the crash-bam-boom stuff you lot like. Evolved on a gas planet, see – combustible weapons not such a clever idea. Oh no, they go for something more imaginative.' The Doctor pointed at the window. 'Like those *things* out there. They're going to destroy the Earth.'

Professor Morris, seemingly oblivious to the tension between Grant and the Doctor, nodded enthusiastically. 'We call them whales.'

'Because of the singing,' Martha said. She'd realised, of course, that it wasn't really whale song when they'd heard it in the TARDIS, but there had been a slow, mournful quality to it that had reminded her of huge yet graceful mammals gliding majestically through the deep.

Except whales were benign, Martha reminded herself. If the Doctor was to be believed, and she would never doubt him, the gas-guzzling creatures floating above the world – *her* world – were anything but.

'Don't you think it's just a little too good to be true?' the Doctor demanded, loud enough to drown out the balloon creature's liquid voice. 'Some alien mob just turns up, out of the blue, offering to put everything right after you lot have wrecked it? I mean, talk about not looking a gift horse – sorry, gift *blob* – in the mouth. How naive can you get?'

'That's enough,' Grant snapped.

'They'll destroy your planet!'

'So you keep saying. Prove it.'

The Doctor grimaced. 'Ah, well here's the thing. I can't actually prove it. Not as such. But give me enough time and I will.'

'Time is something we don't have.' Grant looked pointedly at his watch. 'Now, if you continue to cause a disturbance I'll have you removed.'

'You just try.' Martha clapped a hand to her mouth. The words had come out without her meaning them to.

'Very well,' Grant said, and pressed a button on his watch. Immediately a metal door set into the wall behind him hissed open and half a dozen guards poured into the room. Martha remembered how Grant had been fiddling with the watch when he'd first approached them. They must have been waiting outside all along, alerted by their boss the moment he'd seen her and the Doctor.

The security chief's smile was as cold as space. 'My colleagues will escort you to your quarters. Some rest might calm your nerves.'

The Doctor took a couple of steps back. 'Now, let's not be too hasty. All right, so we didn't exactly get off on the right foot. How about we have a nice cup of tea and a natter, start all over again?'

'Best do as he says, Doctor,' Morris said.

Martha's eyes flicked from Grant and his heavies to the Doctor – who, she noticed, was backing further away from them. She edged towards him, knowing the best place to be in a crisis was at his side.

'You know what? You're absolutely right,' the Doctor answered. 'The only problem is – I'm not very good at doing what I'm told.'

With that he raised one arm, sonic screwdriver in his hand. Its tip glowed blue and all hell broke loose. In a heartbeat the muted lighting turned flashing red and the deafening scream of a siren made Martha cover her ears. She could see Grant barking orders but couldn't hear a word.

Then the Doctor was grabbing her hand, pulling her away. 'Run!'

She didn't need to be told a second time. They raced back along the aisle between the workstations towards the main double doors the Doctor had led her through just minutes before. To Martha's horror, they were slowly sliding shut.

'Come on, faster!'

She didn't think she *could* go any faster, but the thought of being trapped in there with Grant's thugs spurred her on. They sprinted the last few yards and only just squeezed through before the doors closed with a heavy thud.

Had there been any guards on the other side she and the Doctor would have run straight into them, but the corridor was deserted. Martha leaned against the wall, gulping down air, heart thumping. How she envied the Doctor who, despite his 900 years, didn't seem at all out of breath.

He flashed the sonic screwdriver over a keypad at the side of the doorway, fanning the air when sparks cascaded out and a scorching smell filled the corridor. 'Sorry! Smoking – terrible habit. You all right, Martha? Only you look a bit peaky.'

'I'm fine,' she said. Her legs trembled so badly she could barely stand but she didn't want to give him the satisfaction of knowing it, not with his warped sense of humour. 'What did you do back there?'

'Fire alarm – brilliant, eh? I noticed the sensors on the ceiling and knew the doors would close automatically because that's what always happens in the films. But we can't stand here gassing. Remember the way back to the TARDIS?'

Martha recalled the blur of endless corridors, lit by cold white overhead strip lights, remembered the lifts and all those left and right turns that had finally led them here. 'No,' she said with a shake of her head. 'Sorry.'

The Doctor flashed his teeth. 'Don't be! I need to get back there quickly, and I want you to lead Grant's goons away.'

'What do you want me to do?'

'Just keep moving for as long as you can. And stay on this floor – that way you can't inadvertently lead them to the TARDIS. They'll have the doors open before long, so the more time you can buy me, the quicker I can put things right.'

'How bad is it?'

The Doctor stared at her sombrely. 'End of the world bad.'

'Right, well, perhaps you'd better get going, Doctor Smith.'

'I will, Doctor Jones. Try to stay out of trouble.' With that he dashed down the corridor towards the nearest lift.

Martha knew she had to wait for Grant and his men to actually see her if she was going to lead them away from the TARDIS. At least she didn't have to wait long. The Doctor had only just stepped into the lift when the double doors behind her hissed and began to slide open.

'Here we go,' she groaned, and started to run.

'Stop!' she heard Grant cry out, followed seconds later by the sound of footsteps pounding along the corridor after her.

When she came to an intersection she took the corridor to her left, going right at the next one she reached. Martha forced herself to concentrate on running, rather than thinking about what Grant would do when he finally caught her.

Soon her breath was rasping in her throat, her chest was burning and she had to fight to ignore the stitch that flared in her side. If only she could be sure the Doctor had reached the TARDIS by now, she needn't be so worried about leading them away.

'Stop where you are!'

The bellowed command from behind only spurred her on. Walls blurred as Martha, teeth clenched against the pain, raced along the corridor. Now she could hear pounding footsteps closing in on her. Another junction loomed. Martha veered left, crying out when she banged her elbow as she took the turn too quickly.

Ahead she spied a lift, doors open. The Doctor had told her to stay on this floor, but he wasn't the one with a pack of goons on his tail. Martha was certain they'd taken the elevator up to get here, so as long as she didn't go back down she couldn't lead them to the TARDIS.

She staggered into the lift and saw from the display that she was on the thirteenth floor. Bad omen, she thought as she hit the button for the twenty-fifth at random. Shouts made her look round. Grant was leading a handful of guards down the corridor towards her. They were only a few yards away.

'Come on!' Martha screamed at the doors.

'Going somewhere?' Grant taunted.

'Yeah,' said Martha as the doors slid shut. 'Up.'

The last thing she saw before they closed was Grant, face contorted with anger, sprinting towards her. A second later she heard the boom of fists upon metal.

The lift ascended and Martha's spirits rose with it. She'd outfoxed Grant. No doubt he'd be after her as soon as she got to the twenty-fifth floor, but by the time he found her the Doctor would surely have had all the time he needed.

Score one for the good guys, Martha thought, smiling.

The smile disappeared as quickly as her hopes when the lift juddered to a halt, almost knocking her off her feet. Then it slowly descended.

'No!' She jabbed button after button but it made no difference.

Grant must have been able to override the lift. OK, she might as well be philosophical about it. She'd given him a good run and now it was over.

As there was no point trying to escape, Martha decided to play it cool. When the doors swished open, she was leaning against the wall, arms crossed, head tilted to one side. 'Care to join me?'

Grant looked like thunder. 'You and I are going to have a little talk. I'm going to find out what you two are really up to.'

Before he could reach in and grab her, she pushed herself away from the wall and strolled casually out of the lift. 'Come on, then. I haven't got all day.'

The guards looked uncertainly at Grant.

'I'll take her back to control,' he snapped, no doubt furious at having his authority undermined. 'You find that friend of hers.'

Martha could only hope she had bought the Doctor enough time.

'We can do this the easy way or the hard way,' Grant snarled once the guards had stomped off out of sight.

'Very original. For your sake we'll make it the easy way.' Martha turned and, without a backwards glance, began walking along the corridor. Grant swore and went after her. At least he made no effort to grab her, to try to regain some authority by taking control of the situation. Better yet, he kept pace in silence. Only when it became clear Martha was lost did he lead the way. Not that he was taking a risk; Martha knew he'd easily catch her if she tried to run.

The atmosphere in the control centre had changed. When she walked in, all heads turned her way and the looks she was given ranged from suspicious to downright hostile. Even Professor Morris was scowling as he marched up to them, waving a finger at Martha.

'What on earth is going on? And where's Doctor Smith?'

Martha shrugged, realising she could still help the Doctor by keeping silent.

'I have men searching for him,' Grant said. 'He can't hide for ever.'

'I don't understand,' Morris said. 'We're trying to save the world. What could you possibly hope to achieve with all this… nonsense?'

Martha looked away from him, towards the overhead screens.

The Doctor looked straight back at her.

'Hello,' he said cheerfully, giving a little wave.

'What the hell?' Grant's cheeks flushed with anger when he realised the Doctor had hijacked every screen in the room. Martha saw the TARDIS console in the background and sighed with relief. She'd been worried Grant's men might have found him but behind those old doors he was safe.

'Martha, look – I'm on the telly!'

Grant rounded on Martha. 'How's he doing this?'

'You tell me.'

'Now then,' the Doctor continued. 'I suppose you've got a million questions but they're just going to have to wait. See, while you lot were running around like headless chickens, some of us were working.'

'Tell me,' Grant said. 'Or you'll only make it worse for yourself.'

'I don't *know* how he's doing it, all right?' And that was the truth. The Doctor moved in mysterious ways, when he wasn't jumping about, getting all excited.

'And guess what? I worked it all out! Although to be fair, it wasn't that much of a challenge, not for me at any rate. Where was I? Oh yeah, I know.'

The Doctor's face suddenly vanished from the screen, to be replaced by a close-up shot of one of the floating bio-forms. Martha grimaced at the sight of it. The thing was a shapeless grey bubble studded with gill-like protrusions. Various parts of it bulged and then flattened out as it drew in and discharged gases. While there was nothing to provide a sense of scale, she already knew it was huge.

'Now listen,' the Doctor's voice piped up.

A high-pitched keening echoed around the control room, followed by a sonorous rumbling. Seconds later the unearthly duet replayed itself.

'Yeah, I know, it sounds like whale song. But it's not. What you're hearing are encoded signals.'

Morris frowned. 'What's he talking about?'

'One signal goes out from each beastie, transmitting how much gas they've stored up. The other responds with instructions to maintain position.'

'He's insane,' Grant hissed. 'He can't prove anything.'

'Until, that is,' the Doctor said, 'I do *this*.'

The signal changed. The whale song became a harsh trilling. Immediately the creature ceased undulating. Gasps of horror filled the room as it began to sink, slowly spiralling down with its lethal cargo towards Earth.

'My God,' Morris gasped, staring through the window.

Martha looked out and immediately saw something was wrong. The creatures' movements were no longer random. Instead they were drifting in formation across the globe. 'What are they doing?' she asked, not expecting an answer.

'Taking up position,' the Doctor said, striding into the room, sonic screwdriver in his hand. 'They know we're on to them.'

Grant made a move towards him.

The Doctor shook his head sharply. 'Remember what happened the last time you tried?'

Grant eyed the screwdriver and backed off.

'I don't understand,' Martha said, eyes flicking from the Doctor to the screen. It had frozen, and his unmoving face stared back at her.

'That? I recorded it before I left the TARDIS – just added a simple time delay.'

'Yeah, but why?'

'I had to get everyone's attention or Mr Grouch here wouldn't have given me the chance to prove my point.'

'You've doomed everyone,' Grant scowled.

The Doctor rolled his eyes. 'Don't be so dramatic. I just hacked the signal and made one of them think it had been ordered to drop.'

'You killed it?' Martha asked.

'They're not sentient beings, Martha, just big windbags with tiny nervous systems that can only respond to basic commands.' He brushed past them to the nearest workstation. 'That one will come down smack in the middle of the Atlantic. No one gets hurt. Oh, and the creature itself will probably survive, if that makes you feel any better.'

'What about the rest?' Morris was staring anxiously at the creatures. 'It wouldn't take many to wipe out a city.'

'So you *do* believe me! Brilliant!'

'He might, but I don't,' Grant said through gritted teeth. 'That thing only went down because you interfered. Now you've set the rest of them off.'

'You still don't get it, do you?'

'Doctor!' Martha cried. The creatures had suddenly picked up speed and were now racing across the globe.

'All right, keep your shirt on. Those things don't exactly rush.'

'They're rushing now.'

The Doctor glanced out and frowned. 'Clever… they're using the gas to propel themselves,' he muttered, and then started flashing the sonic across the workstation.

Martha said nothing, not wanting to break his concentration.

Morris joined her. The professor flinched as the swarming creatures broke up into clusters of swirling patterns, high above the continents.

Martha looked anxiously at the Doctor. Whatever he was doing, she wished he would hurry up and get on with it. Time was running out.

'They'll hit the cities first,' the Doctor called, eyes fixed on the workstation. 'Kill billions at a stroke and then wait for the gas cloud to finish the rest.'

'Can't the military take them out with missiles?' Martha asked.

'Yeah, except you'd have a massive explosion instead of a burst of lethal gas – not much of an improvement.' He waved his free hand dismissively, obviously trying to focus on what he was doing. From the grim expression on his face it wasn't going well. 'Frequency's constantly changing… can't lock it down…'

Martha chewed on a nail. The creatures were slowing, which had to mean they were getting ready to drop. Far below she could see a shadow over London; her own family would be gone, but she'd have descendants living in the city and she couldn't bear the thought of anything happening to them, or to anyone else, come to that.

She stared at the Doctor but his face was unreadable. He was sonicking like crazy but nothing was happening. Martha felt like screaming.

'Isn't there anything we can do?' Morris pleaded.

The Doctor suddenly smiled. 'You could just ask them to stop.'

'We can communicate with those creatures?'

'Not them! Blimey, for a clever man you aren't half dense at times. I meant those Benefactors of yours.'

'We told you,' Grant barked. 'They're light years away.'

'Are they really?' Now the Doctor was playing the sonic flamboyantly across the work station. 'Thing is,' he said. 'I'd already cracked the code so I only had to lock the signal. Then I could hack into their system. Like *so*.'

Martha hurried away from the window as the space outside distorted.

'Cloaking device,' the Doctor grinned. 'And – oops, guess who broke it.'

The stars disappeared as a gigantic shape shimmered into existence alongside the station. It was a spaceship, but unlike any Martha had seen before – a conical mound of bone-like structures, held together by what looked like a dull greyish resin and dotted with pinpricks of light. There were no engines that she could see. Perhaps they were there but she just didn't recognise them. The ship was big enough to dwarf the station and so utterly alien her mind struggled to comprehend it.

'There you go,' the Doctor said, rubbing his hands together gleefully.

Grant stared slack-jawed at the Benefactor ship.

Even Morris, eminent scientist as he was, was having trouble accepting the proof his own eyes presented. 'B-b-but…' he stammered.

'My thoughts exactly!' the Doctor said, putting one hand on the professor's shoulder and the other on Grant's. 'Every tracking station on Earth will have picked that up. Every nuclear missile you've got will be aimed right at it.'

'What about the gas bombs?' Martha asked. 'Blowing up the ship won't be enough to stop them.'

'It won't get that far – look.' The grey creatures were moving away from the Earth, floating harmlessly into space. 'The Cineraria know they've been spotted. They'll already have detected Earth's defences. Like I told you, they don't do explosions. They do stealth. And I blew their cover. If just one nuke hits them, it's goodnight. So they've admitted defeat.'

Grant was still staring out of the window. 'They're going,' he breathed.

Martha looked. The Cineraria ship was sliding out of orbit.

'What's to say they won't return?' Morris had snapped out of his stupor.

'They don't know about me. As far as they're concerned, it was the human race that beat them. That little mouse has roared. So, no, they won't be back.'

'We were wrong,' Morris said, eyeing Martha and the Doctor. 'Thank you.'

'Just doing my job,' the Doctor said in a bad cowboy accent. Then he turned serious. 'But if you want to thank me, save your planet the hard way.'

'What do you mean?'

'No short cuts, no quick fixes. You don't need anyone's help. The Cineraria think you lot are clever but I *know* you are. You're really quite amazing.'

Martha smiled. She loved it when the Doctor got excited and now he was positively bouncing, hands flying all over the place.

'I mean, you can be stupid and careless,' he went on. 'Look at what you did to the Earth. And yet – and *yet* – there was Newton and Einstein and Hawking and all the others, all those great minds. And all the beauty – oh, don't get me started on that! The Sistine Chapel, the Eiffel Tower, the Hanging Gardens of Babylon—'

'Doctor,' Martha interrupted. Sometimes he needed reining in.

'What? Oh, yeah, sorry. Anyway, my point is, you have the brains and the strength to solve your own problems. The Cineraria didn't completely clear the atmosphere. But they bought you plenty of breathing space. So use it! Finish the job. You're smart enough. And, besides, if you find that gas bag floating somewhere in the Atlantic you can nick their technology.'

'Yes,' Morris said, eyes widening as he considered the possibilities. 'I don't pretend we'll understand it all but I am sure we can extrapolate…'

He was still babbling on when the Doctor took Martha's hand and led her quietly out through the doors. 'Saved the world in less than an hour,' the Doctor said as they headed for the lift. 'I think that's a record.'

'Full of ourselves, aren't we?'

'Yeah, well, you can't blame me. Sometimes I'm so clever I even surprise myself. And it takes a lot to surprise me, I can tell you.'

'Well, you can use some of that genius of yours to take me to Earth.'

The Doctor raised an eyebrow. 'Well, you did it. Surprised me. We've got the whole of time and space to explore and you want to go home?'

'I don't want to go *home*,' Martha said. 'I want you to show me the world ten years from now so I can see how it all works out.'

'Then Earth ten years from now it is. But don't you worry. They manage to sort themselves out, just like I said. Everything's brilliant!'

Martha laughed and slipped her arm through his.

As long as the Doctor was around, everything really was brilliant.

SEVEN

'I can't do it alone,' Martha told the Surcourt group over supper. 'I just can't. I'll do everything I can, but I need help. I need as many of you as possible to become Martha Jones.'

'What?' laughed Sylvie.

Martha grinned and said, 'I mean… do what I'm doing. Get out there and make contact with other groups. Share the stories I've shared with you these past few days. Tell them what's going to happen and what they have to get ready for. Be me, I suppose. Multiply me, so I'm in as many places as possible, spreading the word, and get others to do the same. Be Martha Jones, and make more Marthas.'

'I respect you, Martha, I really do,' said Yves, 'but are words going to be enough? Words and ideas? To beat the Master, we need to fight.'

Several voices murmured in agreement.

'There are all sorts of ways of fighting,' said Martha.

'I mean kill the Master,' said Yves.

'The Doctor—'

'With respect,' said Antoine, 'this Doctor you speak of may be dead already.'

'He isn't,' said Martha. 'I'd know.'

After supper, she helped Mathieu clean the dishes. 'What about you?' she asked him. 'Do you fancy becoming a Martha Jones?'

'Everyone I meet, I'll tell them what you told me,' he replied, 'but I agree with Yves and the others. We should fight. They say the Underground is growing in strength, in the east, in Germany and Switzerland. I've been planning to head that way, to see if I can join them. Maybe I can get the Underground active there too.'

'I've heard people speak about the Underground.'

'There are lots of groups,' Mathieu told her. 'All independent, but if we could link them up…'

'The UCF is strong,' said Martha, 'and the Toclafane…'

'So what else do we do?' asked Mathieu.

'Believe?' she suggested.

Mathieu wrung out the dishcloth and drummed his fingers on the edge of the bowl. Tap-tap-tap-tap! Tap-tap-tap-tap!

'These stories you've told us,' he said, 'of other worlds and alien creatures. Are they true?'

'What do you think?' she asked.

'I think the sky opened two months ago and unearthly things rained down and changed the world. I think anything is possible now. So you've been to these places, to these other worlds and times?'

She nodded.

'The Doctor took you there? What is he really like?'

'He's extraordinary. He never gives up. He never stops fighting. But he always finds the cleverest way to fight. And, believe me, that's never with bombs and guns.'

'Does he know what the Toclafane are?' Mathieu asked.

'No, not yet.'

'Do you?'

She shook her head.

She helped him carry the bowl of dish water over to the grey water recycler and tip it in.

'I can't stay here much longer,' she told him. 'I need to move on.'

'Security's really tight in this zone,' he replied. 'Maybe another month.'

'I can't wait that long,' she said.

Mathieu shrugged and said, 'So we'll find a way, and I'll come with you.'

'There's no need—' Martha began.

'I can take you to other groups between here and Charleville. They, in turn, can link us to others.'

'You don't have to do that,' she said.

'I'm doing it for me,' he said. 'I think it's time I went looking for the Underground.'

'So how do we get out?' she asked.

'I'll think of a way,' he replied.

Griffin and his men were supervising house-to-house sweeps in the suburbs of Surcourt when the call from Brunol came through. Griffin flipped out his phone.

'Speak.'

'Are you looking at the Over Watch?'

'No.'

'I recommend you do, fast,' Brunol said.

Holding the phone to his ear, Griffin jogged past the rows of sobbing detainees held at gunpoint, and headed for his vehicle. Guard dogs stretched on their chains and barked at the frightened captives.

'Shut them up,' Griffin told Jenks.

He got into the cab and pulled up Over Watch on the vehicle PC.

'You seeing it?' asked Brunol over the phone.

'Yeah,' said Griffin.

<Positive make, fugitive Martha Jones. Labour camp in Tournai> the message window read.

'Is this confirmed?' Griffin asked.

'It came through a verified UCF device about twenty minutes ago,' said Brunol. 'I've back-checked. Source says Jones was seen at the camp around nine this morning. Three separate sightings, including one made by a camp guard.'

'That was two hours ago,' said Griffin. 'How far is Tournai from here?'

'It's Belgium. Over the border, about an hour's drive if you push it.'

'Stand by,' Griffin said. He leaned out of the cab. 'With me! Now!' he yelled. His men broke towards him on the double.

Griffin started the engine.

'Brunol?'

'Still here.'

'Clear all the roadblocks and checkpoints between here and Tournai. Warn them we're coming through and we're not stopping. Get the labour camp secured, the labour camp and its immediate location. Mobilise everything you've got.'

'Of course.'

'Brunol?'

'Yes?'

'Secure the camp, but nobody moves in until I'm there. Are we clear? Nobody makes a move for Martha Jones until I'm there.'

'Understood.'

Griffin snapped the phone shut. His men were aboard. He put the vehicle in gear and stood on the accelerator.

'We gotta be somewhere in a hurry, chief?' asked Bremner.

'Tournai. Load up.'

'Yeah?'

Griffin nodded.

'We've got her.'

'As easy as that?' asked Martha, smirking.

Yves nodded.

'Just about,' he said, typing another few words on the rugged PC's keyboard.

<Additional confirmation, fugitive Martha Jones. Tournai labour camp. Request instructions> the screen read.

There was a pause. The network pinged.

<All UCF/Tournai. Hold position and await personnel rendezvous> the new message window read.

The flash market operators had captured the UCF truck during the supply convoy hijack. All the convoy vehicles had been ditched at the warehouse, or dumped in reservoirs and quarries. It would take the UCF a good while to realise that they were missing an ATV that was still active.

'I called in some favours,' Mathieu said. 'Consider this ride a thank you from the marketeers for your warning.'

They loaded their backpacks into the ATV. Dressed in combat boots, army pants and a black leather jacket, Martha said a quick goodbye to the members of the Surcourt group. A wind was picking up, rustling the branches of the elms and poplars that shaded the ruined factory.

'Get indoors, all of you,' she said. 'You shouldn't be out here.'

'God bless you, Martha,' said Sylvie.

'Keep Mathieu safe!' laughed Antoine.

'Remember. Believe,' Martha said, looking at them. She tapped a finger against her temple. 'We'll win this if we remember and believe.'

Mathieu had already given a last wave to his friends and climbed into the cab. 'Martha?' he called.

She opened the passenger door, and looked back at the group one last time.

'Be Martha Jones for me,' she told them, with a grin.

She got in, and they drove away down the road.

The Surcourt group had been good to her. Martha felt an emotional tug as they left them behind, as if she might shed a tear or two at leaving them, but she hadn't allowed herself to cry so far, and she wasn't about to start.

Riding in a UCF vehicle had its advantages. Heading east, through Belsour and Travent-Ville, most checkpoints simply waved them through. The ones that were strict enough to stop them saw nothing amiss with Mathieu's counterfeit pass and paperwork. None of them even noticed that there was a second person in the vehicle.

The dashboard PC, opened in its rubberised casing, flashed them constant updates from Over Watch, enough to forewarn Mathieu on a couple of occasions and allow him to detour UCF mobilisations.

By nightfall they had reached a small village on the Oise, and made contact with the survivor group there. The group helped them conceal the ATV, and then took them to their shelter and gave them beds and a meal.

In return, Martha told a few more of her stories. Some were stories she'd never told before. Others were tales so well rehearsed that they told themselves.

She answered questions and listened to hopes and fears. She told them what she knew, and asked for their help. She urged them to keep the word moving.

She did what the Doctor had asked her to do.

The next day, at first light, rain had set in.

When they started up the ATV and woke the PC, Over Watch was buzzing with alerts. Their ruse had been discovered. Someone, somewhere – the thug with the scarred face, Martha imagined – was seriously raging.

Blanket sweeps had been ordered, border closures, raids and searches.

They drove through the rain towards Rumigny.

'We'll have to ditch this ride soon,' Martha said.

Mathieu nodded.

'We could be carrying a tracker,' Martha said, 'or maybe they can trace our transmissions via the Archangel Net. Trace them right back to this PC.'

'I know. I just want to get as far as Aisonagne, OK?'

'OK.'

They dumped the ATV in a river long before Aisonagne. The rain was sheeting down and the UCF was closing its noose. Helicopter gunships swept the skies, and Martha saw two scudding shoals of Toclafane.

They trekked on foot through rain-swept woods, avoiding the highways, and made it to a place called Veulette by mid-afternoon.

The village was dead. What looked suspiciously like a mass grave lurked in the woodland behind the little school house.

They pushed on, and reached Saint Marcel by nightfall. The rain persisted. A sympathetic farmer, living alone in a stone house on the side of a sloping hill, gave them a ride to Aisonagne in his pick-up. He kept to back roads and field tracks, rolling slowly with his headlights off. The main highways were bright with flood lamps and searchlights.

The farmer dropped them off a mile away from Aisonagne, and showed them the path to take. They reached the town at ten o'clock, and were taken in by a small survivor group that was sheltering in the cellars of the town hall.

There was time for soup and one story, one well-rehearsed story. Martha gave them the quick version of her speech, and hoped it would be enough.

At two, under a moonless night that had only just stopped raining, the Aisonagne group led them through wet fields to the suburban town of Banville.

A much larger group was hidden there, a survivor community nearly seventy strong. Exhausted, Martha did her thing again, cued and encouraged by Mathieu. She'd done it so many times, it was starting to sound stale to her. She hoped it didn't sound stale to them. The congregation seemed to listen, earnestly.

'The Underground? Any of you know anything about the Underground?' Mathieu asked afterwards as they drank bitter coffee and snacked on dry biscuits.

No one seemed to know anything.

'I need to make contact with another group,' Martha told the leader of the Banville enclave. 'I need to keep moving. Can you help me?'

The man nodded.

'We'll have to leave early,' he said.

Early meant four-thirty in the morning. Martha had barely slept. The Banville group led her and Mathieu out into the dark. The rain had begun again, and it was chilly and miserable. Weary and cold to her bones, Martha shivered.

They followed a river through woodland, and passed a huge series of mineral quarries where cranes rose like gangling praying mantises around a half-finished, half-mile-high statue of the Master. It was as if he was looking down at her, his cheeky grin half-complete.

After an hour, the Banville group made signs that they were about to turn back.

'Keep going,' said the leader. 'Follow the edge of the lake around until you reach the road. That will take you into Bassionaire.'

'Is there a group there?' asked Martha. 'A group we can contact?'

'I've sent word to them to expect you,' the leader said.

There were no goodbyes. The Banville group simply vanished into the drizzle and the night.

They trudged on. The rain fell even harder. The track was mud.

'It can't be much further,' Martha groaned.

'Can't it?' Mathieu replied.

Hard, savage lights suddenly banged on. They were blinded. Caught in the floodlights, Martha and Mathieu fumbled around. They heard voices shouting. They heard men moving towards them through the wet undergrowth. They heard weapons racking.

'Down! Get down!' someone shouted.

They got down. Martha saw Mathieu reaching towards his pack. She knew he was carrying a sawn-off shotgun.

'Don't!' she cried. 'Please don't!'

Armed men were all around them, pushing them down, searching their pockets.

It was all over. The UCF had got them.

EIGHT

The chugging Chinook helicopter came pounding in out of the blistering midday heat. It was travelling low and fast, swooping south, dragging its hard, black shadow across the dusty crags and hills east of Izmir.

The pilot said something over the intercom.

'Say again?' said Martha.

'I said not long now, Miss Jones,' the pilot crackled.

She was strapped into a seat on the starboard side of the cabin, gazing out of the window in the hope of catching one last glimpse of the glittering Aegean. It was sweltering hot in the Chinook's cabin, and there were strong fumes from the hastily maintained engine, but it sure as hell beat walking. It was the fastest she'd travelled in four months, and the first time she'd flown since Day Zero. The chopper, a Turkish Air Force bird purloined by the Bulgarian cells of the Underground, was fitted with a transponder that broadcast code-correct UCF transmissions. Even so, they didn't want to stay in the air for too long.

Martha fanned her face and tried to enjoy the experience. It made a change from moving on foot, from lurching trucks and run-down cars, from steamers and container ships, from horseback and dog-sled, from mopeds and the occasional bicycle. She'd even ridden a freight train for two hundred miles between labour camps in the Ukraine.

She'd moved through Europe and the ex-Soviet states to the gateway of the East with the help of the Underground and their whisper channels. She had done her job and told her stories every step of the way.

The Underground wasn't one entity. In the grim weeks following Day Zero, separate resistance efforts had sprung up independently in many countries. Some worked alone, unaware of any similar causes. Others had tentatively linked, sharing intelligence, supplies, weapons, moving refugees and fugitives across borders under the nose of the UCF. Each cell, each group, was made up of the most devoted and determined men and women Martha had ever met. They had put their lives on the line for Martha several times. Five members of the Slovenian cell had died getting Martha out of Ljubljana, and the headquarters of the Munich cell had been raided two days after she'd passed through. All the resistance members who hadn't got out in time had been shipped off to UCF punishment camps in Hungary. Rumours said the Munich raid had been led by a big, scar-faced UCF agent. A cell in Belgrade had been wiped out by the Toclafane the night before Martha had been scheduled to link with them at Kladanj. She'd spent three days on the run in the Trebevic forests, trying to regain contact with the movement.

Her first point of contact with the Underground had been in the rain-drenched night woods above Bassionaire in Eastern France. The Banville group had set the contact up, sending word ahead through their network of agents. Martha and Mathieu had thought that the UCF had cornered them, but it had been the Underground.

The Bassionaire cell had been ready with questions. They'd interviewed them both, carefully. It took them a long while to accept that Martha wasn't a UCF plant sent to undermine them. That entire zone of France had been choked by UCF raids and searches after the Tournai ruse.

Once she'd proved her credentials – her selfless triage efforts following a UCF ambush had helped with that – the Bassionaire cell had taken her seriously. They had links to the East. Messages had been sent back and forth through the whisper channels, city to city, agent to agent. Word was, someone called the Brigadier wanted to meet her. He would be waiting for her at a contact point called Cursus Hill in Turkey.

Mathieu had stayed with the Bassionaire Underground. The last Martha had heard, he'd been heading back to Dijon to help mobilise a cell there.

From the racing helicopter, Martha could see the huge resource plants and mineheads crusting the Aegean coast of Turkey. She could see long, threading caravans of slave labourers, moving to work under UCF escort in the dusty landscape below.

On the outskirts of vanquished Izmir, another monolithic statue of the beaming Master dominated the view. There were effigies of him all over the world.

She'd been told he'd even got himself carved into Mount Rushmore. She decided she'd confirm that when she took her trek to the USA.

It was four months since Day Zero. Her year was a third gone.

The Chinook's engine tone altered.

'Coming in now, Miss Jones,' the pilot radioed, in polite Turkish. 'I won't be able to stay on the LZ long, so I'll say goodbye now. It's been an honour, and I won't forget the things you've told me.'

'Thank you,' Martha replied, adjusting her headset. 'Get home safe.'

'I'll try,' the pilot laughed.

'Will they be there waiting for me?' she asked.

'If the whisper channels have done their job. Stay near the LZ. Contact word is Benton.'

'Benton? *Benton?*'

'I don't make the pass codes up.'

'Right.'

'Good luck, Miss Jones.'

The Chinook dropped sharply. Below them, the dry landscape loomed up, hard rocks and wind-blown crags.

Its blades beating hard, the helicopter settled on a patch of rough ground. The rotors swirled up a huge vortex of white dust.

Martha un-snapped her harness release, grabbed her rucksack, and slid the door open. The outdoor heat hit her, gritty and fierce. She jumped out, and ran through the sand-blast of the rotor-wash, head down.

The silhouetted pilot gave her a thumbs-up from the Chinook's cockpit, and then the noisy bird rose into the air, turning and tilting, nose down, climbing to head for a safe field outside Istanbul.

Martha watched it go, sweat already beading her face.

It flew out of sight. The sound of its rotors dopplered around the crags for a while after it had disappeared.

She was on her own. The sun blazed down. Crickets buzzed in the dry scrub. There was no shade to speak of. Martha pulled out her water bottle and took a swig. She waited. No one came. The dry bowl of crags around her baked in the searing sun.

'You get it?' asked Griffin.

Bremner nodded. Bremner was the intel expert.

'Sweet intercept. Got their chatter word for word, chief,' he said, adjusting his PC. Rafferty looked on, mopping sweat from his forehead.

'Want a playback?' Bremner asked.

'Just the main points,' said Griffin.

'She's set down, right where we thought she would. Her bird is in return passage,' Bremner said. 'Apparently, the contact word is *Benton*.'

'Right where we thought she would,' Griffin mused.

'The Chinook's going to buzz right back over us in a few minutes, chief,' said Jenks. He'd got a shoulder-mounted GTAM out of the truck. 'Want me to spoil its day?'

'No,' said Griffin. 'She might hear the boom. Put that away. Contact UCF Istanbul on the Over Watch and tell them to crump the Chinook when it arrives at their end.'

'Will do,' said Jenks, a note of disappointment in his voice.

They'd spent the best part of three months slowly closing in. It had become a personal quest for Griffin. Rafferty had begun to refer to him as Ahab. The ADC was backing Griffin all the way, but it had become clear from her communications that their Master was increasingly aggravated by Martha Jones's continued liberty.

'Saddle up,' Griffin said. 'Let's go and collect her.'

They got into the waiting jeeps parked on the roasting hill road.

'He's got to love us for this,' Griffin said. 'Martha Jones *and* the Eastern Underground? We're going to blow their net wide open. We're going to give him Martha Jones and the infamous Brigadier.'

'Go!' he ordered. The jeeps kicked up plumes of dust as they sped away.

Martha crunched her way up the dry valley. The sky overhead was an impossible, cloudless blue. The sunlight was so intense, it seemed to anchor down or cancel out any possibility of a breeze. The crickets throbbed.

She entered a village near the LZ. It was a ruin. Trash and debris littered the roads and broken-down houses. She halted as she heard something cough and snort.

The dogs were hungry. No one had fed them in months. Blank-eyed, they moved as a pack, pawing through the wreckage of the world, sniffing for blood.

They'd scented her.

Martha froze, hearing them approach: the skitter of

unclipped claws on stone, the rattle and growl of famished gullets.

The pack rounded the corner of the ruined block ahead of her. It was led by an ugly mastiff that, even in extremity, weighed as much as she did. The dogs began to growl. Foam and spittle dripped from their loose, black gums.

Martha froze, and slid her left hand down the front of her top. As the dogs began to charge her, she pulled out the whistle and blew three hard blasts.

She couldn't hear the sounds, but the dogs could. They scattered, yelping.

It wasn't the first time that trick had saved her life.

'Martha Jones?'

She turned.

A man in black combat fatigues was standing behind her, aiming a pistol at her.

'Martha Jones?' he asked again.

'Are you UCF?' she asked, gripped with fear.

'It depends,' the man replied. 'What's the word?'

'Benton?' she offered.

The man lowered his pistol. He smiled.

'Good reply,' he said. 'Welcome to Cursus Hill, Martha Jones. I'm the Brigadier.'

NINE

There was nobody there. Griffin got out of his jeep and gazed into the heat.

'No one,' Handley reported, running back to him.

'But this is Cursus Hill?' asked Griffin.

'That's what intel said, chief,' said Handley.

'But there's no one here?'

'No one, boss.'

'There is no Cursus Hill, actually,' the Brigadier told her as their truck bounced along the unpaved road. 'It's disinformation. Cursus Hill isn't a geographical location, it's just the code name we give to a meet point. We decide where Cursus Hill is going to be depending on the nature of the operation.'

'I see,' she said.

'You are a high-value target, Miss Jones,' the Brigadier said. 'To our certain knowledge, quite apart from their general security echelons, they have at least three dedicated kill-squads hunting for you. One in particular was closing on your heels in Istanbul, so we had to play things close to our chest. We've changed the location of Cursus Hill four times in the last twenty hours. I imagine the UCF will be cursing your name just about now.'

Martha nodded and said, 'And your name is?'

The Brigadier blinked apologetically. 'I do beg your pardon, Miss Jones,' he said, showing her his credentials. 'I'm Brigadier Erik Calvin, ex-Royal Marines, ex-UNIT.'

'Creds can be faked,' said Martha.

'Indeed they can, Miss Jones. It will be hard for me to convince you of my proper provenance. I merely hoped the fact that we hadn't shot you might have done the trick. My father was a member of UNIT in the seventies. Told me all sorts of stories about the Doctor. He was a bit of a dandy, I hear. They were the days of Lethbridge-Stewart and all that. I thought the *Benton* clue would have been a tip off.'

'I'm sorry,' Martha said. 'I have no idea what you're talking about. Before my time, maybe?'

'Is it? Is it?' Calvin looked crestfallen. 'Oh well, never mind, we've got you now.'

'I'd like to know *who's* got me,' said Martha.

'Oh, the Eastern Underground, of course,' Calvin declared. 'We're the fulcrum, here in Turkey. We link the East and the West: Germany and the Soviet states, India and the sub-continent, China, Norway, all the cells. I was in Ankara on a UNIT posting when it all fell apart. I've been building it up ever since.'

'I see.'

'Miss Jones, I have to ask,' said Calvin. 'You must know. How do we do it?'

'How do we do what?' Martha replied.

'How do we kill a Time Lord?' he asked.

The Underground base was literally underground. Calvin's group was occupying a cave system in the hills, near to the overgrown ruins of an ancient amphitheatre. Camouflage netting disguised clusters of army tents and parked vehicles, but the bulk of the camp was out of the hard sunlight in the cool gloom of the caves.

Walk-boards had been laid down inside the caves, and caverns and side chambers filled with packaged equipment and resources. Lights, strung up along the rough cave walls, ran from small, quiet generators, and power plants deeper in the caves provided electricity for radio sets, a small computer suite, and other technical assets. Martha counted over two dozen operatives in the camp, men and women in dusty military-surplus gear. There were no children.

'Tea?' Calvin asked, offering her a seat at his desk. 'And can you believe…?' He gestured to a plate of digestive biscuits with such an expression of pride, it made Martha smile.

'So you really don't know how it can be done, Miss Jones?' Calvin asked.

'I really don't. I'm sorry.'

'Damn shame,' said Calvin, with an 'oh well' shrug.

'I've never had the opportunity to study Time Lord physiology,' said Martha. 'I have no idea what their weaknesses are. They certainly don't function the way we do and, as I understand it, they can regenerate from even mortal wounds.'

'Yes, frightfully hard to dispose of, that's what I'd heard,' Calvin sighed.

'But you thought I'd know how?' Martha asked.

He nodded. 'I thought that's what you were doing, Miss Jones. I honestly did. From the legend of Martha Jones, traversing the world – and, let me tell you, it is becoming quite a legend – I just assumed that you were searching for something that would do away with the Master. I supposed that the Doctor had told you some secret, told you where to look and what to look for. I thought he'd sent you out to find a weapon.'

'He has, but not in the way you think,' said Martha.

'The Doctor wants the Master stopped, doesn't he?'

'More than anything, but not by killing him. That's not the Doctor's way.'

Calvin raised his hands in puzzlement and said, 'May I say then, I am baffled. With respect, Miss Jones, if you're not a clear and present threat to the Master, why is the UCF so anxious to stop you?'

'I am a threat,' Martha insisted. 'I've got a year to get this right. One year. And if I do, I will end the Master's reign. But I'm not an assassin, and I'm not hunting for some mythical anti-regeneration super-weapon.'

She paused.

'But I suppose,' she added, 'it couldn't hurt if that's what he thought I was doing.'

'Why?' asked Calvin.

'Because that would fit with his notions of what the human race is,' said Martha. 'He treats us with violence and oppression because he expects us to resist with violence. The Master has a low opinion of our species, Brigadier.'

'That much, Miss Jones, is obvious,' remarked Calvin bitterly.

'So, if that's what he thinks I'm doing, fine. Let him think that. I won't contradict him, and it would help me if the Underground kept that rumour in circulation. Anything to distract him from my real purpose.'

'Oh, absolutely,' Calvin agreed. He hesitated. 'And what exactly is that, Miss Jones?' he asked.

They talked until nightfall. As the shadows lengthened in the weed-choked amphitheatre, they walked outside to watch the sun set.

'Will it work?' asked Calvin. 'I mean, will that really work?'

'It has to work,' Martha said. 'If I didn't believe it would, I'd have given up in despair weeks ago. The Archangel communication system is the centrepiece of the Master's control of Earth. It's how he conquered us, how he *really* conquered us, long before the Toclafane came. It's how he made us trust him: rhythmic code, almost hypnotic, and too subtle to hear.'

'I always did wonder how we ever came to elect that blasted Saxon fellow,' muttered the Brigadier, unconsciously rapping his knuckles, Tap-tap-tap-tap!

'The Doctor's plan is to use it against him, but that requires vast preparation.'

'Don't you worry, Miss Jones,' said Calvin. 'The Underground will start recruiting as many Martha Joneses as we can find. We'll get people on the ground, and use the whisper channels too. We'll help spread the word, and get the world ready for the moment of truth.'

'And tell the stories,' Martha said. 'Let me brief some of your people about the sort of stories to circulate. In fact, why don't you share some of your father's tales about the Doctor from the Seventies too?'

The Brigadier nodded.

'We'll tell the stories, all right. And what about you, Miss Jones?'

'Me? I keep walking,' said Martha.

TEN

The bulk container ship *Xin Excel* docked at Yokohama Marine Terminal at eight in the morning, six months after Day Zero.

The climbing sun had turned the uprights of the Yokohama Bay Bridge ice white, and the waters of the bay glowed gold, but a haze of smog generated by ceaseless industrial manufacture hung across the city sprawl, and stained the sky all the way to Tokyo in the north, Chiba in the east, and Kamakura in the south.

Like the rest of the world, the islands of Japan had been enslaved and put to work.

The piers and wharfs of Yokohama's dry cargo docks teamed with activity. Klaxons sounded, ship engines grumbled and snorted like flatulent whales, and shrill loading alarms rang out. Cranes and derricks swung their giant necks around like primordial beasts in the tobacco-coloured haze, and gantry portainers lumbered into delivery positions like catcher crabs. The port was running at a capacity undreamed of in Pre-Day Zero days. Hooting pilot boats and tugs slipped and threaded their way between the moving mass of bulk shipping. Proper safety procedures and docking regulations had long since been abandoned. Schedules and delivery rates were all that mattered now.

The *Xin Excel* was one of dozens of ships bringing in specialist component products and part-assembled materials from what had once been the Russian Federation. Much of this cargo would pass through the specialist factories that had sprouted up like ugly blisters around the edges of Yokohama and Tokyo and then, completed, would be routed back to Russia and China, back to Shipyard Number One and Shipyard Number Four, the largest in the world, where fleets of universe-conquering rockets were being constructed to aim like missiles at the vulnerable heavens.

The *Xin Excel* was also bringing one other valuable cargo to Japan. Her name was Martha Jones.

The only person on the *Xin Excel* who was aware that Martha was aboard was an electrical engineer called Dmitri Korbov. Korbov was an Underground operative from Nakhodka who'd been crewing the run to Yokohama and back since the shipments started, and he used his position to filter whisper channel communiqués in and out of the islands.

'It's different here,' Korbov told her as the *Xin Excel* chugged its way into the crowded port.

'Different how?' Martha asked.

'A different level of security,' he replied, 'a different feel to things. The Underground is far less well established in Japan than in other parts of the world.'

'Why?' she asked.

Korbov shrugged.

'Beats me,' he said. 'There are groups, up in Hokkaido and down south in Kyushu, but Central Honshu, forget it. There are contacts, a few individual operatives, but nothing organised.'

'Because of security?'

He shrugged again.

They were standing at the ship's port rail, looking out across the bustling pier. Two members of the crew strolled past, and greeted Korbov amiably.

'Talking to yourself again, Dimi?' one of them laughed.

'That's right,' said Korbov.

The crewmen looked right through Martha and carried on along the deck.

'All this time you've been on board,' murmured Korbov, 'it still gets me when they do that.'

There were dull thumps and clangs from down below as the *Xin Excel* settled into her berth. Gantry cranes clattered forwards to grasp the first of the containers. Debarkation/handling alarms whooped and buzzed. There would be no preamble or customs delay. The *Xin Excel* would be unloaded immediately, almost prematurely, and then the ship would be sent off again without a pause to gather her breath.

'You've got to remember,' said Korbov, 'the plants here in Japan are about the most high-tech of any in the Master's manufacturing empire. This is what I've heard. We're not talking about gross manufacture like in the shipyards, we're talking about intensive, skill-specific industry. Word is, the Kuro and Shiro plants handle the guidance systems for the rocket fleet.'

Korbov took a slip of paper out of his pocket.

'Your contact's name is Sugu,' he said. 'The address is a worker collective cafeteria near the old bus depot in Kannai.'

'OK,' she said, 'and this Sugu will get me into the labour camps?'

'That's the plan. Eight hours and we'll be leaving again. Eight hours tops. So if you need to get back to me, do it inside that time frame or I'll be long gone.'

'Thanks for everything,' Martha said.

'The only person who deserves any thanks is you,' said Korbov. 'Be safe, Martha Jones.'

No one saw her slip ashore. She hurried through the heaving Marine Terminal, avoiding the work gangs and the trundling bulk loaders with their flashing amber hazard lamps. It was noisy and hectic, the perfect place for someone who was all but invisible anyway to disappear.

The warm air was noxious with smog. It had a dry, petrochemical taste to it. Martha noticed that almost every worker and guard in the terminal was wearing a disposable paper filter mask. As soon as the chance presented itself, Martha helped herself to a mask from an open carton inside the door of a pier office.

The Master watched her progress with indulgent eyes,

his arms folded, his great granite bulk rising above the city from its pedestal in Yamashita Park.

Sugu never showed. Martha never found out why. She loitered around the cafeteria and the adjacent, derelict bus depot for five hours. She felt exposed, even with the perception filter, and hated to have to linger in one location for so long. The longer she stayed, the more likely it was that she would be noticed.

The cafeteria was a steamy, glass-sided place that had once been a popular restaurant. Truck-loads of weary port workers were shipped in from the Marine Terminal every half an hour and fed miserable rations of thin gruel and claggy noodles. UCF guards watched over them, punished rule-breakers, and herded the workers on and off the trucks like sheep.

The depot was a concrete lot, overgrown with weeds. The roof had caved in, and the rusting carcasses of half a dozen public buses lay rotting under the slumped canopy. The place had become the haunt of stray cats. They ran to her, mewing, or hissed at her as she wandered around the ruins.

Martha realised that the cats could see her.

She kept moving, circling the cafeteria, never staying in the same place for too long. She kept praying that Sugu would appear. After four hours waiting, and two heart-stopping moments when she was sure a security guard had noticed her, she vowed to give the contact one more hour.

In the noonday heat, the wretched smog was at its worst. The sky had turned a thick, sludgy ochre colour, and everything was mired in a deep haze. The skyline was so overcast, she couldn't see the mountains. She'd been hoping to see the mountains, but the Master had stolen the view too.

It got hotter. Gloomy thunder muttered in the back of the sky.

Five hours were up. She was going to have to make new plans.

Alone, tense and friendless, she moved through the streets of Yokohama. Terrible damage had been wrought on Day Zero, but Martha noticed there was no sign at all of any Toclafane. She saw a few distant groups of refugees, and found litter-camps in backstreets and underwalks that had been used by vagrant souls.

UCF patrols rolled by with monotonous regularity.

Her original plan had been to enter the huge labour camps serving the Kuro and Shiro plants. She could see the plants from the northern sectors of the city: vast domes the colour of slate that seemed too big and improbable to have been built in six months, let alone set to use. It was amazing what you could accomplish when you had the whole world at your beck and call.

Smaller, subsidiary domes, like metal blisters, surrounded the main plants. There were four of them: Ao, Midori, Aka and Kiiro – respectively, blue, green, red and yellow.

Martha began to work out how she could get into the nearest one.

***

Martha ducked into a doorway. It was late afternoon. Sirens had just started to scream in a street nearby. She heard voices raised in panic, and running footsteps. Then she heard gunshots.

Ragged civilians dashed down the street past her in a frantic search for hiding places. A UCF patrol had surprised a sheltering vagrant group, and was rounding its members up for transportation to the labour camps. Those that ran or resisted were being gunned down. It reminded Martha of South London in the very early days. It brought back her oldest fears and anxieties.

She tried the door she was cowering against, but it was locked. *Just stay in the doorway*, she told herself. *Just stay in the shadows. They can't see you.*

An old man staggered past her doorway, helped along by a teenage boy. Martha winced and looked away as a burst of automatic gunfire cut them down.

Boots crunched closer. Two UCF guards ran past, chasing down the other fugitives. A third stopped to check the bodies of the old man and the teenager.

Stay still. Just stay still. He can't see you.

The guard rose to his feet. He was Japanese. His lean body was packed into black fatigues. His assault rifle was cinched against his chest. He stared into the shadows of the doorway. He stared directly at Martha.

He raised his weapon and aimed it at her.

'Out!' he ordered.

The perception filter wasn't working.

Martha wasn't hidden at all.

ELEVEN

Along with forty other outcasts and refugees, many of them weeping and sobbing, Martha was brought into the Aka Labour Camp just before dark. Martha did not cry.

Black-painted lorries carried them in through the electric chain-link fences, past turrets and elevated guard posts. Inner gates opened and closed as they entered the camp dome. The lorries drew up in a dank concrete bay.

The captives were ordered off the lorries at gun-point, and sent, single file, through processing. Martha expected to be identified at every step. *Martha Jones. Martha Jones. The infamous Martha Jones.*

But she wasn't thumb- or retina-printed, or photographed, or even asked to give her name. No one was. Grimly, she realised that they weren't really being regarded as human at all. They were all just slaves, fodder, fresh blood to keep the engines of industry turning.

The guards took her backpack. She never saw it or

its contents again. There hadn't been much in it, mostly her tools of survival like binoculars, matches and her dog whistle, but in its side pockets, there had been a few irreplaceable keepsakes of her walk: a Polaroid of her with Mathieu and Yves at Surcourt; a Saint Christopher medal she'd been given by a woman in Ljubljana, whom Martha knew had later died so that Martha could live; a little silver Islamic pendant that Korbov had fancied she should take with her; a ridiculous lucky rabbit's foot Brigadier Calvin had insisted on pressing into her hand as they'd said goodbye at another Cursus Hill, telling her, 'My father gave it to me'; and a small plastic badge that read 'Hooray! I am Nine!'

Ironically, the guards didn't take the key pendant from around her neck, or Jack's vortex manipulator strapped in its leather case around her wrist. The manipulator only worked if the Doctor activated it, and it was painfully evident that the key had stopped performing the wonders it had been built to perform.

She was issued with a stale bedroll, a dirty food pail, a colour-coded wristband to denote her work and sleep stations, and a slip of paper printed in eight languages that explained her duties and shifts.

Aka Labour Camp was a huge, high-rise dormitory under the main dome. There were municipal shower blocks at ground level, and above those rose open-grilled, scaffolding decks of tightly packed cages containing metal cots. There was no privacy. Thousands of men and women were packed into the cage city, looking up and down and sideways into one another's miserably confined lives. Sunlight shafted in through the camp dome, tinted into a grey twilight.

Martha's wristband told her she was aka/ao/ten/fifteen. Red camp, blue sector, tenth level, bunk fifteen.

It took her half an hour to find her place and lay out her bed roll. It was weird and uncomfortable. After six months of invisibility, everyone could see her and, as a young, black woman in a predominately Japanese slave force, she really stood out.

She'd barely got into her bunk when hooters sounded and electric cage gates crashed opened.

'Work shift gamma!' the speakers boomed.

She checked her slip. She was work shift gamma. She got up, and followed the others as they filed out.

They were led, in procession, through to Shiro, one of the gigantic plant domes.

Martha looked in awe at the serried decks of heavy manufacture; entire work lines stacked one on top of another, with thousands of workers toiling at fabrication on every level.

She was given her place on deck nineteen. The woman she was taking over from was almost dead with exhaustion.

Martha studied the paper slip. The work was simple enough. As a conveyor belt brought the circuit boards past her, she had to solder two chips into place. She hadn't counted on the speed of the belt. A guard snarled at her for being slow and delaying production. Her hands began to ache from repetition. Ftzz! Ftzz! next one... Ftzz! Ftzz! next one...

She contemplated fusing the chips into the wrong slots until she saw a man dragged off the line two decks down and summarily executed for 'crimes of sabotage'.

Ftzz! Ftzz! next one... Ftzz! Ftzz! next one...

When her shift ended, Martha was numb with fatigue. Her hands were bloody and scarred from slips and solder burns. Replacement workers were led in, and the guards filed her shift back to Aka camp. She had no idea how long they'd been working for. They were given plastic bottles of water, and noodle soup was ladled into their food pails.

She returned to her cot on aka/ao/ten/fifteen. The bunk to her right was occupied by a middle-aged Japanese woman, who was weeping over a lost son. In the bunk to her left was a young man who was so tired he was shivering.

'We're going to die,' he kept mumbling. 'We're all going to die.'

Martha wanted to reassure him, speak to him. She knew she should be telling one of her stories to rally the spirits of the people around her. Though a captive, she knew she should be getting on with her work, but she was too tired.

Fatigue, rather than sleep, swept over her and carried her away.

The next day, and the ones that followed, were all exactly like the first. Martha's production-line skills improved, and she kept her rate up, but every end-shift, she was too tired to talk.

'Where are you from?' the young man in the cot to her left kept asking her.

'Everywhere,' she murmured. 'Let me sleep.'

Her hands were sore and scabbed with burns. There was no sense of day or night. The accumulated smell in the camp was dire. Quite apart from the pitifully poor waste systems, people were regularly dying of exhaustion and malnutrition, and the guards took their time bothering to remove the bodies.

Half-awake, Martha wondered why her perception filter had failed. Had it just worn out?

Every now and then, the hooters would sound as fresh slaves were brought into Aka Camp. Three days after Martha was brought in, a new slave group was going through processing.

'There's been a mistake,' a big Caucasian was telling the guards. 'Look at my creds. Look at them!'

'No mistake,' the guards said.

'For God's sake!' the man yelled.

The guards pointed their weapons at him.

A week had passed. Martha had almost forgotten what proper sunlight looked like. She'd become an automaton. She was very good at her job. Two jabs of the solder, move it on, two jabs of the solder, move it on…

'Will we ever see the sky again?' asked the young man in the bunk to her left. Martha had established his name was Hito.

'Yes,' she nodded, wanting to sleep.

'Will we?' questioned the middle-aged woman in the bunk to her right. The middle-aged woman's name was Tokami.

Martha sighed. She had no strength left, but she summoned something from somewhere.

'Hito?'

'Yes?'

'Call everyone in, everyone from the nearby bunks, everyone who's awake. I've got a story for them.'

'A story?' asked Tokami through the grille.

'I can only tell it once, I'm so tired, but it is a good story.'

Hito gathered about thirty people around Martha's cell. She sat up, weary to the bone, and began.

'Listen to me carefully. I don't know how much longer I can keep doing this, but it's important...'

The Frozen Wastes

When Martha Jones was four years old, she broke her arm. She'd been playing in the park with her brother, riding the swings a little too enthusiastically. She flew off the seat, and for one moment she was actually airborne, it could only have been a split second, and Martha loved it, she was going up and up like an astronaut – and then there was gravity and the ground and dirt and a sharp crack.

'It's not my fault,' said Leo, 'she kept *asking* me to push her harder.' And then he burst into tears.

Martha supposed she really ought to be crying too – after all, she was the one who was actually in pain. But she was being driven to *hospital*, it was an *adventure*, and the whole thing was rather too exciting for tears.

'Nothing to worry about,' said the doctor, 'it's a clean break, look.' And he showed the Jones family the X-rays.

Martha asked if that was really her arm, it looked so strange and ghostly.

'That's what it's like underneath,' explained the doctor,

and smiled at her.

Underneath. It was like a secret world, something which had been hidden from her until that moment.

The doctor told her the arm would have to be put in a cast for a while, 'just to give the bones time to knit back together.'

'You mean,' asked Martha, a little breathless, 'that my arm is going to fix *itself*?'

The doctor nodded. 'You'll be as right as rain,' he told her. 'You're such a brave little girl.'

Martha wanted to tell him that it wasn't bravery at all, it was *curiosity* – but the doctor had been so nice, she didn't want to seem rude.

'I'm going to be a doctor when I grow up,' Martha told her parents that evening over dinner. They smiled and nodded and didn't pay that much attention. They were just relieved her ordeal hadn't upset her too much.

But she didn't change her mind. For Christmas that year she was given a toy stethoscope: it came in a plastic box, and on the cover there was a picture of a little boy trying very hard to look medical. Martha was disappointed that the stethoscope didn't actually work. The nurse outfit her dad gave her was much more practical, and had a girl on the box instead, but Martha found that far less interesting. And books! – so many books, all about how the body worked, what the heart did, the lungs, the blood cells. By the time she was a teenager, and all her school friends had pictures of George Michael on their bedroom walls, Martha instead displayed posters of the human skeleton, each bone arrowed and named. Her mother thought it

THE STORY OF MARTHA

was all a bit grisly, but it was at least better than what Leo
was hanging in his room – he was going through an Iron
Maiden phase.

And each night, with the skeleton gazing down at
her, surrounded by increasingly complex books about
anatomy, Martha would dream. She would dream about
the doctor she would become.

No two children in the world dream the same dream.
Adults do. They get lost in nightmares about mortgages
and internet shopping and having to make speeches in
public. But children don't yet believe the lie that there are
limits to the imagination, and so when they close their
eyes at night there are as many adventures as there are
children thinking them. Take the case of Pierre Bruyère,
for example. In 1868, as a 6-year-old boy, living in a suburb
of Paris, he began to dream of *white*. And once he'd started,
he never stopped. Each time he fell asleep the white would
be there, waiting for him. He didn't know this was unusual,
only that it was sometimes so bright and unforgiving that
he'd wake with a headache.

His parents weren't complex people; they had a little
bakery, all they ever dreamed of was croissants and buns.
'Maybe you're colour blind or something,' said his father.
'Maybe you're just seeing black as white. I don't know.'

Pierre told him that it wasn't *just* white – it was different
shades sometimes, and once in a while it had cracks in.
The father had nothing to say to that. Instead he took him
to a doctor.

The doctor had heard there was some talk on the

continent, in places where doctors could *afford* to worry about such things, that the dreams of a patient might have significance. But this doctor was a gruff sort of man, and told Pierre that dreams were just dreams and there was nothing to be done about them. 'They'll go away,' he said, 'or they won't.'

And Pierre told him he didn't *want* them to go away. 'I like the white,' he whispered in confidence. 'It's mysterious.'

When Pierre was fifteen, an exhibition came to Paris, and his family made a rare journey into the city to see it. Expeditions into the Arctic had been inconclusive at best; the North Pole had never been reached, and yet it still fascinated people – it seemed to Monsieur Bruyère that the entire population of France had crowded into the hall to see the photographs.

'It looks very cold,' said Pierre's mother, rather obviously, 'not very nice at all!'

Pierre looked from picture to picture, at the desolation, at the swatches of snow and ice relieved every now and then by glimpses of the ocean breaking through the cracks between. He could hardly take his eyes off them, and only moved along when an impatient crowd pushed him aside.

'That's what I've been dreaming,' he told his parents.

'You've been dreaming of these pictures?'

'Not the pictures,' said Pierre irritably. 'The *place*. That's what I see when I close my eyes. I'm going to be an Arctic explorer.'

His mother pointed out gently that Arctic exploration was a dangerous career move, wouldn't he be better off baking bread instead? But Pierre was adamant.

As the years went by, it seemed to Pierre that everyone in the world was trying to make it to the North Pole before him. They'd make attempts by boats (which sank), by foot (which frostbit), they'd even come up with new-fangled inventions called *skis*. And every time they failed, Pierre couldn't help but feel relieved. The conquest of the Pole was to be his achievement; he knew it was what he was born for. He felt terribly guilty for a while whenever he delighted in the news of another disaster in the Arctic, of the men who'd perished. And then he forgot to feel guilt any more. He had no room in his brain for such stuff – he had his own schemes to work on. In 1890, he at last addressed a party at the International Geographical Congress in London. He wasn't used to talking in public – he'd been a boy who'd cut himself off from friends – and as a result, he couldn't help but shake as he spoke to the committee.

'Balloon,' he said. 'I'm going to conquer the North Pole by balloon.'

The room was stuffy, and the speakers tedious. In spite of her best efforts, Martha kept on dozing off. The Doctor nudged her. 'This is what we came for,' he whispered.

'They don't even have penguins in the Arctic,' said the Doctor.

There was a crowd to see them off, and stalls for the tourists, selling all kinds of merchandise. There was always a buzz about attempts on the North Pole, and the papers in London spoke of the Arctic season the same way they'd chatter about the Henley regatta. But there was even greater excitement about Bruyère's balloon. Ships are all very well and good and have an undeniable *majesty* about them, but there's nothing as pretty as a balloon, straining against the ropes and the wind for its launch, looking for all the world like an enormous children's toy. 'It's huge,' Martha had said to the Doctor when she first saw it. A ball of pongee silk, the lightest and most resilient material available, it towered above her. Now as she stood in the basket it didn't seem quite so big.

And suddenly they were free. The balloon rose into the air – and it didn't feel to Martha as if they were the ones moving at all. Instead the ground was sucked away from beneath her, the banners wishing them safe voyage, the people waving and cheering and holding up their flags and their rubber icebergs and even – yes – their clockwork penguins. Martha couldn't believe the Doctor was still going on about them. 'Penguins is the *Ant*arctic,' said the Doctor. 'They've got the wrong Pole.'

'Listen,' the Doctor had said to Martha, and so she had listened. Pierre Bruyère spoke to the Geographical Congress, and as he warmed to his subject he forgot to be nervous. He explained how a balloon could cover in a few days distances it would take them months with their dogs and sleds. He wasn't wringing his hands any longer, now he was punching the air with his fist every time he made a point.

'He sounds convincing enough,' Martha had said, a little cautiously.

'Oh, he's brilliant,' said the Doctor. 'You've got to be impressed by the sheer *ingenuity* of it all. All these people trying to explore the Arctic, this man comes at the problem sideways on. I love sideways on. There's really only one problem. Well, one *big* problem. Lots of *little* problems, there are tons of those, of course.'

'What are the little problems?'

'Right. Well, for a start, you can't steer a balloon. I mean, you can do a bit with drag ropes, drop them over the side you get pulled in that direction, but against the Arctic winds? I don't think so, do you? Then there's the gas. At that temperature, you're at the mercy of the sun. When the sun shines, the hydrogen expands, the balloon rises. When it hits a cloud, uh-oh, down you go. And then there's the balloon itself. Cos that's made up of thousands and thousands of silk sheets, all stitched together. Each of the little stitch holes, that's something the gas can leak through, and it will.'

'They don't *sound* like little problems.'

'Nah,' said the Doctor, 'they're pretty small, really.'

'Your tried and tested methods,' Pierre went on, 'they've failed. How many more men will you allow to die? Whereas in a balloon all that's being risked is my life. Mine, and the two crew members I shall need. It's the cheapest, safest means to victory. If I die,' and he shrugged, 'at least it won't be for lack of effort. At least I won't spend my days in a baker's shop, denying my dreams.'

There was silence to that. Martha took advantage of it to whisper to the Doctor. 'OK, so what's the big problem?'

'Well,' said the Doctor. 'He fails. April 1890, he takes off with his crew, he's never heard of again.'

'But, Doctor,' said Martha. 'It's June 1890.'

'Yeah,' said the Doctor. 'Odd, isn't it? We're looking at a

dead man. He just doesn't seem to know it.'

And for a dead man, Pierre Bruyère seemed very animated. 'Gentlemen, you misunderstand me,' he said at last, in exasperation. 'I am not asking your *permission*. I am stating my *intent*. I have already secured funds. I have already found my crew. And we are setting off for the Pole as soon as it is propitious. Good day.'

Martha looked at the Doctor. He gave her a grin. 'Yeah,' he said, 'I know, I know. But you've got to admire sideways.'

Afterwards the Doctor introduced Martha to Pierre. He shook her hand formally. 'I hope we have no need of your medical skills,' he told her solemnly, 'but we have no idea what new illnesses might be waiting for us in such an alien place.' Martha was surprised he didn't comment upon her being a woman. He tutted with impatience. 'It's of no interest whatsoever. If you can do your job, that is enough. We are going to the North Pole, Doctor Jones. I do trust that we will find there more remarkable causes for comment than your gender or the colour of your skin.'

'I don't like him,' Martha said to the Doctor.

'Not the warmest of individuals,' agreed the Doctor. 'Still, I suppose that makes sense where we're going.'

Bruyère hadn't spoken since the balloon had taken off; he'd spent the last three hours making entries in his journal. It would be the record of all their discoveries. It was more important, he explained, than any single member of the crew. Their bodies might fail on their arduous expedition, but so long as it was properly logged, they would live for ever. At last he laid down his pen. 'It's time we ate,' he said.

Open flames weren't allowed in the basket, not with inflammable hydrogen mere feet above. Instead Bruyère had dangled a little stove some thirty feet below the basket, which could be ignited or doused by remote control. There was even a mirror set at an angle, so that if you peered over the side you could see whether the eggs were done yet.

'I told you,' said the Doctor. 'Brilliant.'

Bruyère served up their meals, and they tucked in.

'Gentlemen,' said Pierre at last. 'We are the lucky ones. I am quite certain that the North Pole will be discovered, with or without our efforts. In ten years, maybe, every single place on the Earth will have been mapped, there'll be no need for explorers any more. And Man will have to turn to the skies, and stare at the planets if they want to see anything new. We are privileged. We have been born at the right time, we can still *be the first*.'

Martha had never seen Pierre smile before, but he suddenly did, and it took years off him. Even with his beard, his greying hair, he looked for all the world like a little boy on Christmas morning.

'We're on our way,' he told them. And hugged them both.

Looking back, Martha thought that was the best moment of the expedition, the time that they came together as a team. They sang songs – the Doctor fumbling his way through a Beatles classic, Pierre something very gentle in French that the TARDIS had the sensitivity not to translate. They all peered over the side of the balloon at the sea of ice beneath them, Martha marvelling at how the wind would blow wisps of snow across the surface and make it look like something fluid. Pierre checked his sextant, and announced that in twelve hours' travel they had come further than Nansen's expedition had managed in two whole months. And they all cheered at that, and the Doctor poured them all coffee, and they toasted each other. Pierre sucked on his pipe – 'I can't light it,' he said, 'but I can pretend all the same.'

They set up a sleep rota. It was Martha's turn first. She didn't think she'd be able to get even a wink with the excitement and the brightness of the snow, but she propped herself up against the side of the basket anyway, closed her eyes, and didn't even remember nodding off.

And Martha dreamed that she was going to be a doctor, that was what she wanted most in the world. And no one could stop her, not the girls in the playground, not Leo with his teasing. She'd look at that poster of the human skeleton on her bedroom wall before she turned the lights out, she'd study it so hard that every night she'd dream the names of bones. Hang on, thought Martha to herself, I don't *need* to dream this any more, I *am* a doctor! – but she looked down at her hands and they were so very small, and she was so very young, those ambitions of hers were a *world* away, how would she ever achieve them? And then, suddenly, she was at her exam, the teacher asking her questions and grading her responses. I'm not old enough for this yet, said Martha, and the examiner just smiled. 'Tell me all about the bones, Martha, tell me your hopes and dreams.' So she did, *patella, tibia, fibula*… 'More,' said the teacher, *clavicle, scapula, humerus*, and the teacher put back her head and purred, which Martha thought a very odd thing for a teacher to do. *Ulna, radius*, 'It's so cold out here, Martha, and I must feast to keep warm,' *sacrum, coccyx*, and the teacher tilted her head towards her, opened her eyes wide, and Martha could see they were just shards of ice, glacial like the sea beneath the balloon…

The *balloon*. The Doctor was shaking her. 'Martha, wake up. We've got a problem.' And he didn't pause, he was back to a whirlwind of activity, racing around the basket, grabbing hold of whatever he could, throwing it over the side. Martha squinted through the brightness of the sun, and saw that Pierre was doing the same thing.

'We're still losing height!' cried Pierre. Martha struggled to her feet but it was difficult to find her balance – she could feel now that the balloon was giving way beneath her, she was being pulled downwards fast. She scrabbled about, her hands found the saucepan in which they'd boiled the water for coffee. As she pitched it overboard she was able to see the ground rushing up to meet them. It was impossible to say how close it was, the vast shadow of the balloon stretched out before them like a black smudge on the snow.

'What happened?' she shouted.

'We've jettisoned all the inessentials!' Pierre called out over the wind of their descent. 'What do we do now?'

'Lose the essentials,' said the Doctor. He took hold of a food hamper, strained under the weight. 'Help me,' he cried, and Martha took the other side. Together they staggered with it to the edge of the basket, so unsteady on their feet it looked like they were performing a bizarre dance – and then, 'Now!' said the Doctor, and with a heave, they threw it over.

'Not our food!' Pierre looked ashen. 'No!' He grabbed hold of the second hamper, pulling it away from the Doctor.

'Do you feel that?' said the Doctor. 'Do you feel what's happening?' And Martha could see what he meant, the rate of descent had slowed. 'It *wants* us to get rid of our food.'

'The only force here is gravity.'

'Not that force. The force that's keeping us aloft. We should have crashed on the ice already.'

The bottom of the basket hit a spike of ice, chipping snow over them all. The force knocked them off their feet, the balloon bounced upwards off the impact. 'Next time we'll tip over,' said the Doctor. 'We've no choice.' And they took the remaining hampers, all three of them, and heaved them away.

In that instant the balloon stopped struggling. As if they'd just flicked a switch and turned the crisis off. Oh, the balloon seemed to say, you want me to go *up*? Nothing to it! And with a nonchalance that almost made Martha laugh, calmly, lazily, it began to rise once more into the air. They gained height quickly – Martha watched all the provisions dwindle to the size of ants against the snow, then disappear completely.

'We're alive,' she said. It was obvious. But it needed to be said.

'Whatever this thing is,' said the Doctor, 'it wants us

entirely at its mercy.' He stared at the polar wastes ahead of them.

One day Pierre looked up from his sextant, cleared his throat formally, and announced that he thought they must nearly be there. 'Below us, gentlemen, is the North Pole.'

Martha couldn't help herself, she looked over the side of the basket. It was a pointless thing to do, and she knew it was pointless. Nothing but white below them, white above them, nothing but white all around. Nothing but white for weeks.

'What do you think, Doctor?' asked Pierre. But the Doctor hadn't spoken for a long time.

At first the Doctor had been characteristically exuberant. 'We have to stay alive,' he told them, 'that's what matters. Gather everything which we can throw overboard, just in case we need ballast again.' Martha even thought he was enjoying himself as he arranged the heaviest items around the perimeter for easy access. Sledges, scientific instruments. 'We've got to be prepared to junk the lot,' said the Doctor. He took hold of Pierre's journal, but the explorer snatched it back. 'Not that,' said Pierre, and for a moment it looked as if the Doctor would argue, but then he nodded, let go. 'No,' he agreed. 'All right. Not that.'

They made sure they kept warm, and took regular turns to sleep and keep watch. Not that there was anything to watch. After a few hours Martha found the stark blankness all around her almost blinding. There was no food, of course, and the Doctor told them they'd have to cope as best they could. That day Martha hadn't felt hungry anyway, she supposed she was too scared. And after a couple more days she stopped questioning it, and by the end of that first week she'd even forgotten she *should* be hungry. Once in a while her thoughts would drift, and she'd wonder about it – wasn't there something she should be doing with food, she'd think dreamily, shouldn't she be *eating* it, something like that – then with a jolt she'd realise she should be starving. No, really, literally starving. And then she'd feel dozy again, and the voice in her head would tell her not to worry about it. OK, she'd tell the voice, and give in to sleep – I'm sure if anything *were* wrong, the Doctor would take care of it.

Sometimes Martha's dreams would be peaceful. She wouldn't remember what they'd been when she woke up, but they'd been all hers and nobody else's. But more often than not they'd get interrupted by that woman examiner. 'Never mind that holiday in Bermuda,' she'd say, 'never mind that Christmas when you were seven, never mind that date with Leonardo DiCaprio. Tell me about the bones, Martha. It's so very cold, I must feast. Tell me all about the bones, and why you love them so much.'

When they'd run out of songs, the crew began to share dreams. Martha told the Doctor and Pierre how she had always wanted to study medicine. And Pierre told them his dreams of white.

The Doctor hadn't paid much attention to anything in weeks, Martha had been getting very worried – but at this he showed a sudden interest. 'Nothing but white, really?'

'But out here,' said Pierre, '*amongst* the white… sometimes I now dream of other things.'

'What other things?'

'Just other things,' Pierre would shrug. 'Just not white. As if I've been set free. It's a relief.'

Pierre wouldn't say much any more either, he liked to sleep as long as possible. He'd do so with a grin across his face, and look so at peace that Martha would feel envious. And when he was awake he'd be scribbling in his journal. Martha couldn't see why. Nothing was happening for him to write about. But he'd write anyway, one arm hiding it from view, as if he didn't want anyone to copy his homework.

'What do you dream of, Doctor?' asked Martha.

'I don't dream,' he said shortly.

But one time, when Pierre was asleep, he told Martha.

'On old maps you'll find the words "Here Be Dragons". It doesn't mean there really *were* dragons, of course. Only that there were places no one had ever been. They didn't know what they'd find, there could be anything. Explorers like Pierre, they don't think that's good enough. They keep pushing against the limits of what they know, they refuse ever to sit back and say, that's enough. They won't give in to the dragons. But,' he said, 'what if, when you get out there, into the unknown… you find there are dragons waiting after all?'

One day Pierre looked up from his sextant, and said that they must nearly be there. 'Below us, gentlemen, is the North Pole. What do you think, Doctor?' But the Doctor just looked at him grimly.

'How can you tell?' asked Martha. 'We can't even see land.'

'We've been travelling at a steady rate of twenty knots

these past two months. Always on the same course, the winds have been constant.'

'Wait a moment,' said Martha. 'These past *months*? How long do you think we've been travelling for?'

Pierre frowned. 'Four, maybe five months. What's your estimate?'

Martha felt like laughing. 'That's ridiculous. It can't be more than a fortnight.'

'What do you think, Doctor?' asked Pierre again.

Martha looked at her old friend. 'Yes, Doctor, how long have we been doing this?'

The Doctor licked his lips. Spoke quietly. 'It's been years. Years and years, I lost count. So many... I've tried to shield you from the worst of it, took so much concentration. I'm sorry.'

His companions looked dumbly at him.

'Entire lifetimes, crouching here in a basket. And yet,' he said, and took out his sonic screwdriver. Martha had never been so pleased to see something so safe, so familiar. The Doctor pointed it over the side of the balloon, aimed downwards. A blue light pierced through the white, it lost none of its intensity as it burned ever downwards, illuminating the way. And hundreds of feet below them... shapes to make out... yes! Martha could see the snow. And the ice. And the hampers of food they had jettisoned.

'And yet,' continued the Doctor, 'it's been no time at all.'

'They're not even frozen over,' said Pierre, hushed. 'They'd have frozen over in *minutes*.' He looked up at the Doctor, and his face was suddenly livid, and Martha thought he might actually hit him. 'It's impossible! That's the North Pole below us! It *has* to be. And I shall write as much in my journal!'

'Your journal is nothing but lies.' But Pierre stomped over to the book anyway, sat down, and picked up his pen.

'What is it, Doctor?' asked Martha.

'It distorts time,' said the Doctor. 'Running the same seconds back over and over. We're literally frozen in them. The perfect larder. Where the meat stays fresh and never runs out.'

Pierre couldn't speak. He tried, but the words just didn't come out, his mouth opening and closing like a goldfish. So he had to pass his journal to the Doctor dumbly. The Doctor looked inside. All the pages were filled. They'd been filled many times over, one diary entry over another over another, until all the words were illegible, a mess of black ink.

'I don't think this is your first expedition to the North Pole,' said the Doctor. He handed the journal back to Pierre, who dropped it listlessly to the floor. 'Let's find out.' He raised the sonic screwdriver high and, as he pushed down just once, there was the smallest of beeps – and the giant gas balloon above them popped open. There was a whoosh of hydrogen into the arctic sky, so dense that Martha could actually see it, and then the silk covers that had kept them afloat fell away and were lost in the white. Martha steeled herself for the fall, the inevitable crash upon the ice below – but, ridiculously, they just *hung* there in mid-air. She looked down, but the ground just sat there, out of reach, stubbornly refusing to obey the laws of physics. And then she looked up.

She'd not been able to look upwards for so long. The balloon had been her sky, it had blocked out everything else above them. And now she could do nothing but gawp. The Doctor and Pierre were already doing the same.

They were not alone.

Balloons. At first Martha thought there was a dozen of them, and that was impossible enough – but then she saw there was a layer above that, and the layers kept going on and on – there were *hundreds* of balloons, maybe thousands, a whole flotilla of them blotting out the sky. And that wasn't the strangest thing of all.

'They're *my* balloon,' said Pierre. 'The same insignia, the same design…' And there he stopped, because he didn't dare carry on, he knew if he said it aloud his mind might crack – but the same *Pierre* too, standing at the edge of each basket, flanked always by two different crewmembers.

'What did I do?' he heard himself ask.

'What's been done *to* you,' corrected the Doctor. 'It's caught you in a loop. Each time you set out with companions, and each time it sends you back to the beginning for new ones. The same polar expedition over and over, always doomed to failure.'

'But why?' asked Martha. 'What possible reason could it have to do that?'

'All it can do is eat,' said the Doctor. 'That's all. And so it's everything humanity isn't. Because you all have aspirations, desires, the urge to reach out and be something greater than you are. And that's what it feeds on. Human ambition. The very thing that makes you think or feel. It's obscene.' He turned to Pierre. 'It's reached into your very dreams, made you want to be an explorer, made you hunger to come here again and again.'

Pierre's face was an agony. 'Are you saying that all that desire I had to explore… to add to the sum of human knowledge… it wasn't even mine in the first place?'

The Doctor said nothing, because he had no answer to give.

Pierre wobbled on his feet, he looked as if he might faint, he grabbed hold of the edge of the basket to steady himself. And then he gripped it harder, his knuckles flared, and he shouted out into the frozen wastes.

'I wanted to be somebody special…' The ice bit at his face and made his eyes water. 'Come to me,' he said. 'Come to me right now, and tell me I'm not to my face.'

The Pierre Bruyère in the balloon above tilted its head in what looked like consideration. Then it shrugged. It sat itself upon the edge of the basket, and swinging its legs over the side, lowered itself down. Soon it was hanging there only by his fingernails, some nine metres above the real Pierre Bruyère's head. It looked downwards, seemed to tut in irritation to see how far it still had to go. And then the fingernails *grew*, they stretched out like elastic, only it wasn't elastic, it was *ice*, they'd become ten long icicles and Pierre was dropping gently into the basket beside them.

'How much of me is really me?' one Pierre asked the other bravely. 'Could I ever have been a great man at all?' His counterpart was speckled with frost like icing sugar, his hair frozen to his head, his teeth chattering, his eyes hard flint. 'I'm so cold,' this Pierre said, almost apologetically, and with something like tenderness brought his hands up to the other's cheeks, and drained the life out of him.

'My turn, I think,' said the Doctor. And the Pierre Bruyère monster turned away from the frozen corpse he had created.

'I've felt you buzzing away around my dreams. You want to know what's inside, don't you? You want to know my hopes and desires, where *I've* explored.' He stepped closer; the ice cold of Pierre's face didn't even change expression. 'I've navigated the North West Passage, stepped on the moon, been to Mars, Venus, planets you'll need three tongues to pronounce. I've sipped tea on the rim of burning constellations that were lost millennia ago. And I'm not done yet. *I'm not done yet.* So, if you want to feast, you'd better be hungry.' And he didn't wait, he grabbed hold of Pierre's hands, drove them into his cheeks, and held tight.

The white darkened. Turned red. Turned purple like a bruise. 'Can you feel it?' gasped the Doctor. 'All those dreams you'll never know. That you'll never understand.' And he cried out. 'Martha, I made a mistake. I thought I could weaken it, could fill it to bursting. But it's so cold, and it's so hungry.'

And Martha didn't hesitate, she put her own hands upon the Doctor's cheeks too. She felt how cold they were, and she was so warm against them, and she pushed harder until she could feel she'd reached the Doctor's warmth too, she knew it must be deep inside somewhere.

'And I've been to the moon too,' she spat in Pierre's face.

'I've not sipped tea at half so many constellations, but I've sipped at a good few. But that was never my dream. I'm not an explorer. I just wanted to put people back together again.'

There they stood, the Doctor and Martha, clasped together, embracing the monster. And with a dull crump, the sound of a footfall in heavy snow, time unfroze, flung backwards, and the wounded sky burst like a berry.

And one day Martha did visit the North Pole.

'We never did get there, did we?' asked the Doctor. 'What with everything else going on. Well, soon fix that!' He set the controls, gave the pump a particularly vigorous workout, and a minute later he opened the doors. 'Bit parky out there,' he said. 'Won't stay for long.'

Martha stepped out into the snow. She hugged herself against the cold. She looked at the white, stretching out in all directions.

'It's just a place,' she said at last.

'Just a place,' the Doctor agreed. 'Sometimes the destination isn't half as interesting as the ambition to get there.' He pointed at where she'd left footprints. 'Look at that. It's 1890, give or take a year or two. You're the first person to have stood at the North Pole. Martha Jones, pioneer!'

She laughed.

'Come on,' he said. And before they left, he smeared away their prints carefully. 'Don't want to spoil it for anyone else. Let's go and get something to warm us up.'

He took the TARDIS to exactly the same place, a mere

two hundred years later. The North Pole Experience was an interactive museum, with exhibits that the children could play with, and a gift shop filled with 'I've Been to the North Pole' T-shirts and clockwork penguins.

'Still don't have penguins in the Arctic,' said the Doctor.

He bought them both overpriced coffees in the café, found them a nice table in the observation lounge, and they looked out the plastic windows at what had been the most isolated place in the world.

And he told her what he dreamed. How, on his planet, the maps never said 'Here Be Dragons'. Because his people had explored the universe, they'd been everywhere and everywhen. At one moment there they'd been, charting the stars, and the next, it was all over. That was time travel for you. When he'd been a child, the Doctor had wanted to be an explorer. But there was nowhere left to discover. They told him he shouldn't leave home, what was the point? But he'd found a point. He'd found a point. And whenever he forgot it, he'd close his eyes, he'd dream again, and there it would be.

Pierre Bruyère never got to visit the North Pole, of course. When he was 6 years old he complained to his parents, 'I never dream of anything. When I sleep, nothing happens.' Everybody else dreamed, what was wrong with him?

His parents took him to a doctor. 'Dreams are a nuisance,' he was told gruffly. 'You're better off without them.' Privately the doctor was annoyed that he'd been bothered by something so trivial. He's the son of a baker, he told himself. What great things was he ever going to dream about?

So Pierre worked in his parents' shop. He never smiled.

'Put a bit of love into it,' his mother advised him gently, 'that's what I do.'

But Pierre couldn't see what there was to love about croissants and baguettes and Belgian buns that would never even see Belgium, they'd never explore as far as even that.

One day Pierre made a pastry. He sprinkled on the icing sugar. He looked it over. Needs more sugar, he said to himself. He poured on another layer, then another. The little flecks of white covered the bread, covered the counter, his hands were speckled with white. After he'd used three entire bags of icing sugar, and drowned the pastry completely, he wondered why he'd done that.

But that night he began to dream again. Just flashes of white, little glimpses of it, and what he could be. And he began to smile at work, to look forward to the rest at day's end. Once in a while he'd feel inspired to cover pastries so thick with cream you'd think that it had been snowing. And sometimes he'd make buns in the shape of balloons, so light and fluffy you could almost have sworn they could rise up to float in the air.

TWELVE

Her nerves were frayed and her exhaustion was fathomless, but Martha was quietly pleased to discover that her story had hit a nerve.

'They all want another, tonight,' Hito told her through the mesh.

'I don't know, Hito…'

'Oh, please, Martha.'

'I'm so tired,' Martha groaned.

'We're all tired,' said Tokami.

'Your story's already spreading though Aka,' said Hito.

'All right, all right,' Martha said, sitting up on her bunk. 'I'll tell another story tonight, but you have to promise me you'll bring workers in from other sections. I need to get the stories to spread and sink in, you understand?'

'Yes, Martha,' said Hito.

Martha lay back on her metal cot again, hoping to grab another half-hour's sleep. She realised there was someone standing in the doorway of her cage. She looked up.

A big man with a scarred face was looking down at her from the doorway. It was the same scar-faced man who had chased her across Europe and the Middle East.

Martha gasped and scrambled back into the corner of her cage.

'Martha? What's the matter?' asked Tokami through the cage wall.

'It's him. It's him!' Martha hissed.

'Hello, Martha Jones,' said Griffin. 'We meet at last.'

Griffin sniffed, folded his arms, and leaned casually against the door frame.

Martha didn't move.

'I heard you were here, so I thought I'd introduce myself,' Griffin said. 'The situation being so… ironic.'

Martha didn't answer. She stared at him, and past him, into the walkway. Where were his men? Where were the armed UCF squaddies to back him up and drag her away?

She swallowed. The scar-faced man was alone. Was he intending to simply finish her himself, then and there?

'Don't you think it's ironic?' he asked. Martha didn't reply. The man nodded to himself. 'I had a hunch you might not be particularly chatty with me.'

'You spent six months pursuing me across the face of the planet,' Martha said quietly. 'You've tried to kill me. What do you expect?'

'Fair point,' the man replied. 'My name's Griffin, by the way.' He showed her his UCF identity card. 'What happened to your fancy perception filter?' he asked.

She said nothing.

'You lose it, or did it break down?'

She remained silent.

He shrugged.

'I'm only making conversation,' he said.

'Just get it over with,' said Martha.

Griffin stared at her. 'You think… you think I've come to kill you or something?'

'Or drag me off to the Master,' she said.

'If only,' Griffin snorted. 'Sorry, Martha Jones, I thought you'd realised.'

'Realised what?'

Griffin showed her his colour-coded wristband. 'I'm a prisoner too, just like you,' he said.

Martha stared at him. 'What are you talking about?'

Griffin sat down on the far end of her cot. 'I'm a prisoner. A labour slave. A raid patrol picked me up and brought me in a few days ago.'

'Stop it,' said Martha.

'Stop what?'

'This is some kind of trick. A ruse to wrong-foot me. You want information or something.'

'No. Honestly, no.'

'I don't believe you,' said Martha. 'You're just trying to get information out of me. You'd have just shot me or extracted me to the *Valiant* otherwise.'

'I'm telling the truth, woman,' said Griffin.

'Rubbish! You're UCF! You've got the credentials to prove it—'

'Yeah,' mused Griffin, looking at his ID, 'the guards here don't seem very impressed by that.'

'Why would the UCF lock up one of their own?'

'It's a puzzle, all right. I can tell you, I was surprised,' said Griffin. 'There's only one explanation I can think of.'

'And what's that?' asked Martha.

'The UCF isn't running this place. The guards might wear the uniform, but they don't answer to the Master. Someone else is in charge here.'

THIRTEEN

It was another two shifts before she saw Griffin again. He found her waiting in a post-shift food line, queuing for a ration of noodle soup.

'Thought any more about what I said?' Griffin asked.

Martha ignored him.

'Oh, stop it with the cold-shoulder treatment, Jones. Really, it's getting old. I understand that we're never going to be friends, and we have a history on the outside. But in here, in Aka, we're just another couple of lost souls. And something's going on here.'

'I don't know what you expect me to say or do,' Martha replied.

'Listen to me for five minutes,' he suggested.

'For the last six months,' Griffin said, 'all I've wanted to do is catch you. There was a lot riding on it: big promotions, the favour of Our Master.'

'Yours maybe, not mine.'

Griffin shrugged. 'Anyway, things have changed. Right now, I personally don't care what happens to you. I just want to get out of here alive. And I reckon being trapped in here is kind of messing up your mission too.'

Martha looked at him, mocking.

'What? So we team up and escape? Is that what you're suggesting?' she asked.

'You put it like that, it sounds stupid,' said Griffin, 'but I reckon my chances of getting out of Aka will be a whole lot better with you on board.'

'Why?'

'Because you're the famous Martha Jones, and for Our Master to want you quite so badly, you must be a serious operator.'

They were sitting in her cage and eating their meagre food.

'Go on, then,' Martha said. 'Five minutes.'

'There's something going on here. Our Master doesn't—'

'If you're going to mention him, just call him the Master,' Martha interrupted. 'This "Our" business makes my skin crawl.'

Griffin nodded, and dredged the soup with his spoon. 'Whatever's going on here, the Master doesn't know about it. He's not aware of it. To the outside world, Japan is just another part of the global empire. It's covered by the Over Watch net, and administered by the UCF, just like everywhere else.'

'Go on.'

'I tracked you through the Russian Federation. Our last

brush was at Shipyard One, remember that?'

She nodded sourly.

'You gave me the slip, as usual. Slippery Martha Jones. But I had a number of good leads. That's the thing, Martha, you go around the world telling people who you are and asking them to remember you, you leave a trail.'

'I said go on.'

Griffin smiled. 'I was pretty sure you were heading to Japan by ship, and I wanted to jump ahead and be waiting for you. Now, to move from zone to zone, you need authorisation, even if you're UCF. So I contacted UCF Coordination Japan, and requested permission to bring my team into Honshu by air. They turned me down. According to them, this is a no-fly zone, because of the sensitivity of the work being done in the plants. You see any Toclafane here?'

'No,' she admitted.

'UCF Japan informed me that even Toclafane are banned from their airspace, something about their energetic profiles adversely affecting the guidance systems under manufacture. The only way in or out is by sea. Doesn't that sound a little suspect to you?'

Martha frowned. 'It seems excessive. But then, there's something odd here. When I got close to the Kuro and Shiro plants, my perception filter failed. That's how I was caught.'

Griffin nodded, interested. 'I got in touch with my ADC,' he said. 'She's one of Ou- *the* Master's sector chiefs. I asked her to pull some strings, maybe even get the Master to order UCF Japan to allow a plane in, and even she ran into a brick wall. UCF Japan told her that my intel was wrong. Martha Jones was not coming to Japan. They said they had positive data placing Martha Jones on a supertanker heading into Ch'ongjin in North Korea. I was advised to route my team that way.'

'But you thought better?' said Martha.

'I *knew* better, Jones. I may have spent six months failing to catch you, but I know how you work, and I've learned to read the traces. Japan was wrong. I told my ADC so and firmly but politely suggested she sorted it out. More dragging of heels. I was losing time. You were getting away. So I took a leaf out of your book, Jones.'

'You became a nice person all of a sudden?' she asked snidely.

'Ha ha. Funny girl. I stowed away. I jumped on a supply ship heading for Yokohama, following your trail. I took my oppo, Bob Rafferty, with me. I left the rest of my team in Vladivostok, waiting for the go command from my ADC to fly in and join me. Far as I know, they're still there, kicking their heels.'

'As far as you know?'

Griffin put his food pail down on the cage floor. 'When I got here, my direct phone link to UCF High Command stopped working,' he said. 'It's Archangel, but it stopped working. I lost contact with my team, the *Valiant* and my ADC. My special little phone broke down, Jones, just like your filter.'

Martha dropped her spoon into her pail and waited for him to continue.

'The five minutes are almost up, Griffin,' she said.

'Me and Rafferty had been on the ground here six hours when the patrol rounded us up. We showed them our credentials. They weren't interested. Rafferty tried to impress upon them that we were legitimate UCF. They shot him in the head, execution style. No warning, no caution, just a double tap. That's when I realised that things weren't right in Japan. Not right at all.'

'And you surrendered?'

Griffin frowned. 'I'm a soldier. I know about killing, and I'm not ashamed to admit it,' he said. 'The men in the raid patrol had a look in their eyes. Sometimes you fight, sometimes you know when to fold your hands behind your head.'

He looked up at the cages stacked above them. They could both hear sobbing and moaning. Somewhere, someone was shrieking with pain or frustration. Guards were shouting. The stench of Aka, though they had grown used to it, was dispiriting.

'This may not be the best situation in the world,' Griffin said, 'but I'm still alive. And so are you. You believe in hope, Jones?'

'Do you have to ask?' she said.

He smiled. 'This is what hope feels like, when hope is all you've got.'

Her belly empty, her hands shaking, Martha dragged herself through the next shift on deck nineteen of Shiro dome. She burned the ball of her thumb badly with her solder gun, and a guard hit her twice in the ribs for delaying the belt rate.

As she settled back to the demanding, monotonous toil, her ribs throbbing, Martha realised that her Aka slave existence wasn't just another trial she was being forced to endure. It wasn't an experience she could drive herself to live through and afterwards look back on. This was it. They were going to work her until she died. Unless she did something about it, Aka labour camp and Shiro work plant were going to be her life until it ended.

If her life ended here, then the world ended with it. Her task was only half done. The world was waiting for her. The Doctor was counting on her. So were her mother and her father…

She refused to cry. If she cried, she'd miss a circuit board on the belt, and that would mean another beating, or worse.

She thought about Griffin. She thought about hope.

She thought about a little girl who was looking after her earrings.

Martha had begun to set up a pattern for her storytelling. The guards noticed if too many people shifted around in the cage decks between shifts, so she scheduled things carefully: a three-night pattern. Hito, and another boy called Ono, would bring a group of slaves to her on the first night, and other slaves, ones who had already heard her speak, would filter out and take their places in the cages. On the second night, Martha would rest, and the slaves who had heard the stories would spread out through the cage decks and communicate them to groups of their own. On every third night, Martha would furtively leave her cage and go and talk to a new group on a different deck.

'I'd like to hear one of your stories,' Griffin said to her in the food line.

'Don't. Just stay in your cage,' she told him.

'But—'

'Griffin, if you want to earn my cooperation, you'll start doing what I tell you.'

Griffin nodded, but he was beginning to hear the stories anyway. Jones was good, he had to give her credit. She fired people up. Once they'd heard her speak, they couldn't help sending her stories on. One by one, second hand, he was hearing most of them.

Martha flopped down on her cot. It was shift end, and she felt brain-dead with fatigue. Her hands were wrapped in dirty bandages, most of them strips torn from her bedding. The Aka guards didn't care how much the work damaged her. There was no first aid or medical functionary.

Hito appeared in the doorway of her cage. It was story night. She was due to perform.

'Hito, please, give me ten minutes,' she sighed.

Hito shook his head. 'Tonight's listeners aren't here yet, Martha Jones,' he said. 'You have time to rest.'

He came into her cage, and made a quick, respectful bow. He'd reserved a portion of his ration for her again. Hito kept doing that, no matter how many times she gratefully made him take it back for himself.

'Hito, I thank you, but please…'

'I've heard something, Martha Jones,' he said. He bowed again.

'What sort of something?' she asked.

'I have heard that there is a third plant, Martha Jones. Yuki heard, and told Basu, and he told Ono, who told me.'

She sat up. 'A third plant? What does that mean?'

Hito shrugged. 'There is Kuro and there is Shiro, and there is a third plant. It is called Koban.'

'Koban?'

Hito nodded, eagerly.

'Aka and Kiiro slave camps service Shiro, Ao and Midori camps service Kuro. But there is also Koban. Yuki heard, and told Basu, who told—'

'Get to the point, Hito, please,' she begged.

'Every month,' said Hito, 'the guards come and extract workers from Aka to serve at Koban. Thirty workers every month. They pick them at random, if no one volunteers.'

'But you can volunteer?' she asked.

Hito nodded. 'This is what Yuki told Basu.'

'What is this Koban?'

Hito made a face. 'That, I cannot say. But they claim it's a way out of the camps.'

'Why?'

'Because none of the workers ever come back.'

'None of the workers ever come back,' Martha said.

Griffin thought about that.

Martha felt extremely uneasy standing in the doorway of Griffin's cage. It felt like she was appeasing the enemy.

'They claim it's a way out of the camps,' Martha added.

Griffin nodded. 'None of the workers ever come back. What does that say to you, Jones?'

'It suggests that none of the workers ever come back because they're dead.'

'Exactly.'

'But what if none of the workers ever come back because they're moved to a facility with better conditions? You know, as a perk of taking on extra responsibility?'

Griffin shrugged.

'Still sounds like a bad idea to me, Jones,' he said.

Martha sagged a little. 'Me too, I suppose.'

Griffin looked up at her. 'You were thinking of going for it?' he asked.

She sighed and said, 'I don't know. Possible death is preferable to certain death, isn't it? Isn't that how a soldier like you would calculate it?'

Griffin sniggered. 'Sounds too rich for my blood,' he returned.

'So what? We stay here until they work us into our graves?'

He rose to face her.

'I've been looking around,' he said. 'Looking for weak links in the security. I think I've found a few places that are compromised. Early days, Jones, but frankly I'd rather try to break out of here, a place I know, than risk getting into a worse situation.'

She nodded. 'I just thought I'd tell you,' she said.

'You're going to do it, aren't you, Jones?' Griffin asked.

'I haven't made my mind up,' she replied. 'Probably not. You're right. You're right. Aka is bad, but the grass may not be greener.'

***

Hooters sounded. Sirens wailed.

'Koban! Koban! Any takers for work duties in Koban plant!' the guards shouted. 'Volunteers? Better conditions! Privileges! Complete a two-week tour in Koban, and you earn your freedom!'

None of the slaves made a move. They stared down out of their cages.

'All right then,' announced the chief guard to his underlings. 'Pick them by numbers and generate a work crew. Thirty workers!'

The camp guards consulted their manifests, and started yelling out numbers.

'I volunteer,' Martha called out.

The chief guard nodded, and gestured to Martha.

'Good. Down here, please.'

'I volunteer too!' shouted Hito.

'Join the line, slave,' the chief replied.

As Hito ran up behind her, Martha turned to glare at him.

'No, you don't!' she hissed. 'Don't do this!'

'I go where you go, Martha Jones,' Hito said, grinning.

'Oh, please, don't do this to me,' she groaned.

'I volunteer!' Ono called out.

'So do I!' cried Tokami.

'No! No, no!' Martha growled.

'So do I,' said a voice. Griffin clumped down the grilled stairs from his cage to join them. 'Anywhere's got to be better than here,' he told the guards.

They forced him into line. He nodded to Martha. She didn't know whether to feel pleased or angry.

Once the guards had filled their quota of thirty bodies, they opened the gates of Aka camp.

A school bus, repainted in UCF drab black, was waiting for them in the dank concrete bay. They filed aboard. Hito seemed almost jubilant. Griffin avoided Martha and sat at the back alone. Tokami took the seat beside Martha.

'Where are they taking us, Martha, do you think?' Tokami asked.

Martha didn't reply. She had a terrible feeling of foreboding. Taking herself over the precipice was one thing. Taking innocents with her was quite another.

The bus started up and drove out of the bay. The gates of Aka camp opened to let them out.

They drove for an hour. For a fraction of a second in that hour, Martha glimpsed the mountains, peeping through the sickly smog.

Koban plant was a grey concrete block twenty storeys tall, surrounded by rings of pain-wire and auto-gun emplacements. Five cage gates opened and closed to let them in. They drove down a long ramp into a basement garage, where the guards ordered them out.

'It smells funny in here,' Hito said.

'Quiet!' one of the guards ordered.

'Kid's right,' Griffin whispered, coming in close behind Martha. 'The air's wrong. Something's off.'

'Prepare for sanitisation!' the chief guard yelled.

All notions of dignity were abandoned at that point. Faced with aimed guns, they were required to strip and walk through a series of harsh, pungent chemical showers. At the far end of the shower block, they were blown dry by air systems, and handed overalls by hazmat-suited personnel.

'This isn't promising,' Griffin whispered to Martha as he pulled his overalls on.

'Just look somewhere else until I'm dressed,' Martha replied.

A hatch opened.

'In here,' ordered one of the hazmat guards.

A large antechamber awaited them on the other side of the hatch. It was bathed in cold, silvery light. The guards withdrew and closed the hatch.

'Welcome to Koban, volunteers,' voices said in unison. The words sounded clipped, as if the voices weren't used to speaking the language.

'Who are you?' Martha called out.

'We are in control here,' said the voices, mingled as one, 'and you are the famous Martha Jones.'

FOURTEEN

The Relativistic Segue occupied a vast chamber in the heart of the Koban plant. The chamber stank of electromagnetics and ozone. The Segue was contained within a framework of polished chrome obelisks rooted on a stone plinth. The design of the obelisks, even their proportions, revealed that though they had been constructed from terrestrial materials, they had not been designed by a terrestrial mind.

The Segue was like a bright bolt of lightning moving in very slow motion. It was an artificially induced tear in the fabric of space-time. The Drast were very proud of it.

They were also fascinated by Martha Jones.

'You are the famous companion of the Doctor,' said one.

'Tell us about the Doctor,' requested another.

'Tell us about the Master,' added a third.

'Tell us about the Time Lords. Tell us the secrets they have told you.'

They had removed her from the volunteer group, and taken her to an observation platform overlooking the Segue. There were six of them, and they gathered around her inquisitively. They were tall, slender and vaguely humanoid, though their anatomical proportions seemed wrong. Each one wore a suit of complex, tight-fitting armour made out of a gleaming blue metal, and they covered their faces behind extravagantly ornate metal masks that reminded Martha of squawking birds. A bright tungsten light shone through the eye and mouth slits of the masks, and from gaps between the closely wrought segments of their armour, suggesting that their bodies were bioluminescent, like creatures of the deepest, darkest limits of the ocean.

'Who are you?' Martha asked.

'We are the Drast,' said one.

'We are Drast Speculation Initiative Fourteen,' said another.

'What does that mean?' asked Martha. 'How long have you been on Earth?'

'One Earth decade,' said another.

'And what is your purpose?' she asked.

'We are Drast Speculation Initiative Fourteen,' they repeated.

'What does that mean?' Martha asked.

'We were sent by the Great Drast to conduct a clandestine assessment of this world,' one of them replied.

'We were further charged to initiate economic takeover,' another added.

'You're... invaders?' Martha asked.

'We are speculators. We despise warfare. We engage with the economic infrastructures of chosen worlds, and manipulate them until effective cultural and economic control of the chosen worlds are ours.'

'You mean you take over the running of entire worlds without anyone knowing?' Martha's eyes were wide.

'It is a long and complex operation,' said a Drast.

'A successful speculation may take generations to complete. Subtle micro-adjustments are made over a period of years to engineer crucial measures of control,' said another.

Martha shook her head in disbelief. 'Are you telling me that when the Master took control of the planet, it was already being invaded?' she asked.

'The arrival of the Master was an unforeseen variable,' said one of the Drast.

'We cannot compete with him. He would obliterate us. This Speculation Initiative has been abandoned,' said another.

'We have used disguise fields to conceal ourselves from the Master while we arrange and execute our withdrawal from Earth,' said a third.

'You mean get in your spaceship and fly away?' asked Martha.

'Use of conventional inter-system craft is not an option,' one of the Drast answered. 'The Master would obliterate our craft before we had cleared the atmosphere.'

'Our withdrawal from Earth,' added another, 'must therefore be accomplished using the Segue.'

***

The Drast, Martha learned, had been well established in Japan's technology sectors when the Master had revealed himself. They had used their position to clandestinely take control of the guidance manufacture operation that the Master had set up in Honshu. This allowed them access to some of the most advanced technology that the Master was developing for his fleet, including the potent Black Hole Converters.

One such converter had been partially dismantled in the Koban plant, and then activated under laboratory conditions. It had opened the Relativistic Segue. It had torn a hole in time and space, a doorway through which the Drast could escape.

It wasn't that simple, of course.

Martha watched from the platform as armed guards in hazmat suits led one of volunteers into the Segue chamber. It was Ono. The boy looked scared. He had a harness buckled to him, from which ran a safety line. The guards walked Ono towards the Segue plinth, the line playing out behind him.

'I don't understand,' said Martha, with mounting concern.

'The Segue must be calibrated until transit is safe,' said one of the Drast.

'The Segue could lead anywhere,' said another. 'Into the heart of a sun, into empty space, into a toxic world. It must be tested. If the test result is deemed unfavourable, the Segue is recalibrated to a new location and another test is made.'

'Tested?' Martha breathed. 'By... by sending someone through it?'

'This is the most effective way of testing.'

'But you can't!' she cried. 'This is what the volunteers are for? You just can't!'

'But we can.'

'And we have.'

'And we are.'

Martha looked on in horror as Ono nervously approached the incandescent split of the Segue. He took one last glance behind him and stepped into the light.

He vanished. The safety line slowly began to drag into the Segue at waist height.

'How many times have you done this?' Martha asked.

'Ninety-eight times,' said the Drast.

'And how many times has it been... unfavourable?'

'Ninety-eight times,' said the Drast.

'So ninety-eight volunteers have been killed?'

'It is impossible to determine. Few have been retrieved. None has been retrieved intact.'

The safety line suddenly went slack and dropped to the ground. The guards hauled on it, pulling it back out of the Segue. Ono was no longer attached to it. The end of the line was fused and smouldering.

'Test ninety-nine complete,' announced one of the Drast.

'Result deemed unfavourable.'

'Begin recalibration of the Segue.'

'Prepare another test subject.'

***

'They're going to send us through a hole in space one by one until one of us comes back alive?' asked Griffin.

'That's the idea,' Martha replied. She had been returned to the volunteer group in the holding room.

Griffin shook his head. 'Just when I thought the world couldn't get any crazier,' he said.

'What did they want with you, Martha?' asked Hito.

'They wanted to find out what I knew about the Master. They're afraid of him. I think they assume that, because of my connection to the Doctor, I must know of secret weaknesses they can exploit. They wouldn't be the first to think that.'

'What did you tell them?' asked Tokami anxiously.

'Nothing,' Martha replied. 'When I saw what they did to Ono, I wasn't in the mood to answer questions. I expect I'll be summoned again later. They're busy recalibrating the Segue.'

'What will you tell them then?' asked Griffin.

'Nothing,' Martha snapped.

'We've got to get out of here,' said Griffin. 'We've got to find a way out. Fight our way out, if necessary.'

'Fight?' echoed Martha. She looked around the group of scared volunteers. 'I think you're the only fighter here, Griffin.'

He shook his head. 'Everyone's a fighter if they have to be,' he told her. 'I say we rush the guards next time they come for one of us.'

'No,' said Martha.

'It could work,' said Griffin. 'They're probably used to people being too cowed and freaked out by this place to offer any resistance. We rush them and—'

'No,' said Martha.

Griffin scowled at her. 'So we just sit and wait for them to walk us to our deaths, one by one?' he asked.

She hesitated. 'No,' she said. 'I'm going to talk to them. I'm going to tell them something.'

'What?' asked Griffin.

'A story,' she said.

'I would like you to listen to me,' said Martha. 'I know you're afraid of the Master. You have every right to be, but you are advanced beings. You have amazing technology at your disposal. Your technology has already proved capable of fooling the Master.'

'What is the purpose of this dialogue?' asked the Drast.

'I'm saying to you that you could help,' she said. 'You could help me, you could help the Doctor, and you could help the human race. If we work together we could overthrow the Master.'

'This outcome is unfavourable,' one of them replied.

'I'm not saying it will be easy,' said Martha. 'I'm asking you to help the human race in its darkest hour.'

'This outcome is unfavourable,' said another.

'If we stand together, we could make a difference,' she said. 'It's what the Doctor would do...'

Star-Crossed

There were six of them – no, seven, Martha realised. She was just able to make out the seventh man, in the gloom behind the others. The passage was too narrow for them to stand more than three abreast and the lighting strips set into the low ceiling were only putting out a weak, flickering luminescence.

The men were armed with an assortment of crude weapons: metal bars, strips of metal sharpened into ragged-looking knives. One of them, Martha noticed, was brandishing a large spanner, as if he had raided a toolbox before joining the others.

'Let her go,' one of them said. He was tall and powerfully built, his hair cropped short. He wore a plain grey coverall that had been patched in a couple of places.

From what Martha could make out in the poor light, the others in the group were equally well built and wore similar coveralls, each bearing their own pattern of stains and repairs.

The man behind Martha said nothing, but took a step back. The painful way he held Martha's arms twisted up into the middle of her back meant that she had no choice but to take a step back, too.

On the floor between Martha and the armed men, the Doctor eased himself up off his knees. As he straightened, he gingerly pressed his hand against the base of his skull.

'Well, now that was unexpected,' he said.

He had been standing with his back to Martha, facing the armed men who had come pounding along the corridor, shouting for someone called 'Breed' not to move.

The only other person in the corridor was the lone, unarmed figure who had half-run, half-stumbled into them a moment or two earlier; this, Martha assumed, must be Breed.

Seeing the weapons in their hands, the Doctor had stepped forward, smiling. He'd spread his arms and his long coat formed a curtain between the armed group and their quarry.

'Hello! I'm the Doctor. Maybe I could—'

That was when Breed had hit him – a single punch, hard, at the base of his skull. Martha didn't need her medical training to know that punch could cause some serious damage. The Doctor had dropped like a puppet whose strings had been cut.

The next thing Martha knew was that someone was behind her and had hold of her arms and, if she tried to move them, they hurt. A lot.

'You think that's going to stop us?' The leader of the armed group spoke again.

The grip on Martha's arms shifted, eased for a moment, then tightened, just as an arm slid across her throat. It suddenly became much less comfortable to take a breath.

'OK, that's enough. Hold it right there!' the Doctor said. He was on his feet and his voice had taken on a harder edge. 'Before anyone gets hurt and I have to do something I might regret.'

Everything seemed to happen at once. The armed men lunged forward as if they were a single animal, teeth bared, weapons poised to strike. Martha felt the arm clamp more tightly across her throat. She choked, struggling for breath as she was dragged backwards, away from the Doctor and the armed men who now seemed to be having trouble getting past him. The Doctor seemed to have tripped and stumbled into the path of the armed men and, however much they shouted at him and whichever way they tried to get around him, they just couldn't get past. As she was hauled along the corridor, now moving so quickly that she was running backwards on tip-toe, held up by the same arm that was choking her, the scene receded into the gloom.

Grey mist edged her vision. For a heartbeat she felt as if she was floating, held up by the bubble of her last breath. Then the bubble burst and she was falling.

'Oops. So sorry. Clumsy old me.' The Doctor lurched suddenly across the corridor. The armed gang tried to push past him, but somehow he was always in their way, arms out, pushing them back as he righted himself, only to lose his footing yet again and flounder back into their path.

The gang's leader swore and jabbed his makeshift blade at the Doctor but found himself clutching air. The weapon had vanished.

'Is this yours?' the Doctor asked innocently as he offered the knife to another member of the group – who hardly had time to shake his head before he was holding the knife and the metal bar he had been carrying found its way into the hand of one of his companions.

'If you hold this and I give this to you, then I can take that and give it to you to look after….' Words cascaded from the Doctor as the men's weapons moved from hand to fist – at one point, a particularly thin and wicked-looking blade seemed to be plucked from behind its erstwhile owner's ear – apparently under some mysterious power of their own. Like the captive audience of an insanely gifted illusionist, they were unable to keep a firm grasp on their weapons until Breed was…

Gone. The Doctor glanced down the now-empty corridor and stopped, back on exactly the spot he had been standing when the men first lunged forward.

'So,' he said, hands now jammed in his pockets. 'Which one of you's going to take me to your leader?'

The coffins were racked in tiers around the walls, linked by thick skeins of wiring and flexible tubing. The dim lighting threw deep shadows across the cramped space. Glasses on, the Doctor was peering at the readouts displayed on a bank of screens at one end of the racks. He jabbed at a screen, tapped another and watched columns of figures scroll down them. Martha watched him, nagged by the intense feeling that she had been here before.

'What's this – some kind of outer-space freezer aisle?' she asked, her sense of dislocation intensifying. She had said that the last time she was here.

'Very good!' The Doctor laughed as he clambered up a clanging metal ladder and raced along the first walkway. His head bobbed as he glanced at the smaller screens bolted to the foot of each coffin. 'These caskets are cryogenic units. Built to last, too.' He kicked the nearest coffin, producing a deep, hollow tone.

'Cryogenic,' repeated Martha, who was beginning to feel she as if she was reciting a rehearsed script. 'So we're talking suspended animation then?'

'Exactly!' The Doctor had reached the end of the walkway. He slid down the ladder and bounced over to Martha. 'Whoever lay down in one of these caskets wouldn't have expected to wake up for a long time. Decades. Centuries even.' He whipped off his glasses and waved them in the air as he paced back and forth. 'I'd bet my shirt that this is a generation ship. But I wouldn't bet my shirt because it's a very nice shirt and I wouldn't want to lose it. Only I wouldn't – lose my shirt, I mean – because I'm right. I mean, how often have you known me to be wrong?'

'Rewind a second, will you?' Martha said, even though she knew what the Doctor's answer would be, before she asked the question. 'Generation ship?'

'A tin can full of frozen colonists. Whole families fired at the world they're going to colonise and more or less forgotten. Until they reach their target world, when the cargo's thawed out and woken up so they're able to get on with being explorers and colonists instead of frozen meat products.' The Doctor looked around the dimly lit racks of empty caskets.

'The caskets aren't drawing any power but, judging by these readouts, I'd say power's running low all over the ship. It's still a long way from its target. And the cargo should still be asleep.'

The Doctor should have spun on his heel and marched out the door, but he leaned in close and stared deep into her eyes. The intensity of his gaze made her gasp and catch her breath. He was so close, she could reach out and—

'Are you all right?' he asked. There was something wrong with his face. It was bloating, losing shape – no, changing shape. She opened her mouth to warn him… and discovered that she could not breath.

'Are you all right?' the Doctor repeated. Mouth gaping like a landed fish, Martha thought it must be pretty obvious that she wasn't all right. But the Doctor continued to stare at her, and his face continued to change shape, skin running like hot wax, one eye ballooning while the other changed colour.

'Are you all right?' It wasn't the Doctor's voice now. Female. Coming from a lipless mouth in a face without form. Martha's struggle for breath became a struggle to scream.

'Are you all right?' the monstrosity repeated. 'Please tell me you're all right!'

Martha coughed and took a deep gulping breath. The face above her snapped into shape and focus: a young woman.

'Are you all right?' the woman asked. 'Please tell me you're all right.'

Blinking, eyes adjusting to the dim light, Martha saw a second face, looking down at her: Breed.

'I know you,' she croaked. She pushed herself backwards across the rough metal floor, panic rising.

Martha's back hit something and she froze. Looking back and up, she saw a face. Breed's face.

Barely suppressing a scream, Martha recoiled, scuttled round on the floor and somehow got her feet under her. Springing upright – and fighting to keep her balance as her head swam and her stomach lurched – she desperately scanned the dimly lit space for an escape route.

Smaller than the cryogenic chamber, it was crammed with storage tanks, connected by a maze of ductwork and cables to a series of caskets racked against one wall. The caskets' full-length hatches hung open and Martha became aware of a damp, mouldy odour that came from their direction.

But most of her attention was focused on Breed, who stood a short way in front of her, when he should have been behind her. And on the group of ten or so other figures, fanning out around the cramped space, surrounding her.

They all wore Breed's face.

The nutrient troughs had been roughly welded together from metal sheets scavenged, the Doctor assumed, from all over the ship. They ran the length of the empty hold and the pale, grey-veined foliage of the hydroponically reared crops hung limply over their sides.

'Human beings,' the Doctor said with a grin. 'You really are brilliant! A situation might look hopeless, but that doesn't stop you trying to do something about it.' He shaded his eyes and looked up at the light-strips that hung over the troughs.

'That doesn't answer my question,' said the man who had introduced himself as Treve, Chief Planetary Surveyor and ad hoc head of the Steering Council. Laine, the leader of the armed group that had been pursuing Breed, stood beside Treve, having reported the events in the tunnel. Two of Laine's group now flanked the Doctor. Treve noticed they looked nervous, kept shooting sideways glances at the prisoner, as if they expected – feared, almost – he might make some sudden move.

'Eh?' The Doctor stopped staring up at the light strips and returned his attention to Treve. 'Oh. Right. Your question… Which was…?'

'Who are you and where's the Breed designated Theta-Nine?'

'That's two questions and I've already answered one of them. I'm the Doctor. I told your man there – you called him Laine when he frogmarched me in here – when we met in the corridor, but he seemed more interested in putting my friend's life in danger.'

'You're the one who got in our way,' Laine said. 'For all I know the Breed grabbing her was some kind of bluff to get us to hold back.'

'And he'd already clobbered me for what – a bit of a laugh?' The Doctor's tone was mocking. 'I just have this thing about bullies. You know, the type who gang up on someone and go after them like a pack of dogs. Don't like them. Don't like them at all.' He paused, before going on: 'Still, I imagine it must have come as a shock, waking up and finding that you were still light years from your new home.'

Treve blinked, as surprised by the sudden shift in the prisoner's tone from menacing to breezy as by his apparent knowledge of the onboard situation. 'How…?'

'Oh, the empty cryo-caskets, the energy readings – you're still in deep space, so there's nothing for the solar arrays to collect – and your DIY hydroponics. Raided the seed store, the stuff intended to cultivate the new world? Like I said before: drop human beings in a tight spot and they'll improvise like mad to get out of it. Give you lot lemons and before you know it, you're passing round the lemonade!' The Doctor went back to squinting at the lights.

'Exactly how hard did Theta-Nine hit him?' Treve asked.

'Harder than we thought, from the sound of things,' Laine replied.

'So tell me.' The Doctor was brisk. 'How long since you came out of cryo-sleep?'

'A little over two years,' said Treve. 'Luckily, the cryo-system malfunctioned during a scheduled maintenance cycle. Artificials had been decanted and were performing their programmed tasks. They re-tasked to revive as many of us as possible.'

'As many as possible?'

'About half,' Laine answered. 'Funny how that evened

out the numbers nicely.' There was an edge of bitterness to his voice.

'You lost someone?' the Doctor asked.

Laine nodded. 'My wife. Both my children.'

'I'm very sorry. I know what it's like to lose someone you care about.' The Doctor paused, lost in thought for a moment, then asked: 'Breed is one of these *Artificials*? What are they? Genetic clones, vat-grown and stored, then woken up to perform regular maintenance checks or to deal with any small emergencies? I'm guessing there must be some cybernetic augmentation, so the ship can wake them up when needed?'

'You know a lot about Breeds for someone who claims not to be on their side,' said Laine.

'I know a lot about a lot of things,' the Doctor replied. 'This isn't the first time I've encountered the use of clone slaves. I gather that Breed isn't a name. It's a description.'

Treve nodded. 'Bottle-Breeds.'

'Charming.'

'Their purpose is to maintain the ship and protect the cargo. The same basic personality profile is loaded into each one upon activation,' Treve said. 'They're essentially the same person.'

'Except one of them isn't. What has Theta-Nine done to deserve being chased by an armed gang?'

'He calls himself Edison,' said the man to the Doctor's left.

'Edison?' the Doctor asked, eyebrows raised.

'They started changing their designations,' said Treve, 'and illegally accessing the ship's historical database to choose new ones.'

'Names!' The Doctor laughed. 'They've chosen names for themselves instead of anonymous old Theta-This and Gamma-That. Doesn't sound like something a basic personality profile would do, does it?'

'Artificials were never intended to have such extended run-times,' the guard to the Doctor's left cut in again. 'The basic program is adaptive – to enable a Breed to react to changes in a situation. Running for two years, the basic program has made larger and larger adaptive leaps, and…'

The Doctor finished the guard's explanation for him. 'And the mass-produced drones have become individuals! I'd have thought that studying the development of a new form of intelligence would be much more interesting to a cybernetic systems expert than acting like a thug.'

'How did you know…?' The man shrank back.

The Doctor parroted Treve's earlier words. '"You know a lot about Breeds for someone who claims not to be on their side." But that doesn't answer my question: what has Edison done for you to want him dead?'

'You fell in love?' Martha was incredulous. 'They want to kill you because you *fell in love*?'

'They were more interested in compelling me to reveal Romea's whereabouts,' replied the man who Martha had, until a few minutes ago, thought of as Breed. There was something in the smoothness of his tone and his choice of words that hinted at his language having been downloaded into a chip-enhanced brain rather than learned during a natural childhood. 'I would have resisted their efforts to extract this information from me, so the outcome would almost certainly have been my termination.'

Martha noticed the young woman squeeze Edison's hand as they moved ahead of her along the corridor. In front of them moved the rest of the Breed – Artificials, Martha reminded herself – from the decanting unit. That cramped, slightly smelly room was where Edison and the rest of them were grown and stored. The mouldy smell, Martha had discovered, came from the last of the growth fluid, which had curdled in the curved bottoms of the growth tanks.

Martha had been peering into the grey/brown sludge at the bottom of one of the vats when a weird flutter seemed to go through the Artificials, as if they were stalks of identical corn being moved by the breeze. Suddenly they were heading out the door, led by an Edison lookalike who had introduced himself as Byron. There was a Jason, a Curie and a Demosthenes in the group, too, Martha had discovered as they introduced themselves – once she had stopped hyperventilating at the sight of ten identical copies of the creature she believed had kidnapped and almost killed her.

They approached slowly, as if trying to calm a frightened animal, then the young woman – Romea – had stepped forward to explain and apologise for Martha's rough treatment. Edison hadn't intended to hurt her, but Artificials were stronger than humans – they had to be, as there was no heavy lifting machinery on board. 'Not yet, anyway.'

'Artificials are forbidden from fraternising with colonists,' Edison continued. 'The rules are quite clear.'

'When they thought you were just part of the ship's self-repair system, they didn't mind who you spent time with,' Romea said, then turned to Martha, smiling shyly. 'I'd already begun to get to know him. I knew my father wouldn't approve, so we met in secret.'

'When not on duty, all Artificials are to confine themselves to the decanting unit,' Edison recited as he walked. Martha thought she could detect a bitter edge to his voice. 'Artificials are to refrain from all non-technical conversations with colonists…'

'Artificials are to pretend to be machines,' Romea added. 'That might have been how they were designed, but now they're individuals.'

'But your father and the other colonists don't accept that?'

'The colonising families were chosen for our genetic superiority. We all have the DNA markers for physical robustness, good immune response, intelligence. All the things you'd want if you were founding an outpost on a new world. The Steering Council believe our genetic purity should be preserved, no matter what the cost.'

'Sounds ominous. How far do you think they'd go to get you back?'

'It's gone beyond that. There was talk of reprogramming. Some people were suspicious that so many of the colonists had died during the cryo-system failure. They thought the Artificials had decided to make sure we didn't have the strength of numbers. The systems techs tried to access the ship's cybernetic system and download a virus to wipe out the adapted personalities, but the system had been locked.'

'We may be artificial, but we're not stupid,' said Edison.

Martha couldn't help but chuckle.

'That's when they started talking about rendering,' said Romea. 'And that's when I knew I had to pick a side.'

'Rendering?'

Romea nodded. 'Once an Artificial had completed its scheduled maintenance duties, it would enter the rendering vat. The body would be returned to its constituent amino acids and recycled to grow another Artificial.'

Martha looked at Edison. 'So you're…'

'Grown from the recycled bodies of those who came before me,' Edison confirmed. 'We all are.'

'Somehow I can't see you all queuing up to jump into the rendering vat now.'

'No. That would require force.'

'But Artificials are stronger than humans. Get yourselves some knives and the colonists will have lost their advantage. They'd have to talk.'

'The colonists want firearms, beam weapons,' Edison said. 'If they are the first to acquire them, they will soon be loading our corpses into the rendering vat.'

'You mean this ship has guns but no tractors or fork-lifts? That's crazy!'

'The fabricator can make them all, weapons and tractors,' said Edison. 'But if they activate it, they'll kill everybody.'

***

'A fabricator?' The Doctor sounded dubious. 'Your energy reserves are already low. Activating a fabricator would finish them off entirely. You'd be left in the cold and dark until the solar panel arrays could collect enough sunlight to recharge the batteries. You'd freeze and suffocate on your own CO_2 before you had enough power to turn on a light!'

'We only need to run it for a very short time. Long enough to produce the weapons we need.' Treve's tone was steely, determined. 'The Artificials' enhanced strength gives them an unnatural advantage—'

'So you want something that goes shooty and bang-bang to tip the balance of power in your favour,' the Doctor cut in. 'Even if it dooms you all?'

'This debate is at an end,' Treve said with a thin smile of triumph. 'Our people are on their way there now. They will secure the area and activate the fabricator. I'm satisfied that you are no threat to our plans, so I will join them. You will stay here, under guard, at least until we have dealt with the Artificial problem.'

Suddenly the Doctor was a blur of motion, leaping at Treve before either of his guards could react, passing through the narrow space between Treve and Laine and vaulting the hydroponics trough. The pale, ill-nourished plants rustled drily as he brushed past them. Two long strides brought him to another trough, which he again hurdled, passing between the plants like a breath of wind.

'Stop him!' Laine bellowed.

The two guards hesitated, unsure whether to follow the Doctor over the trough or take the long way around the trough-ends. The Doctor had already hurdled the third trough and he ran on, jumping through the forest of malnourished plants until he vaulted the last of the troughs and found himself facing a blank metal wall.

To his left was a metal stairway leading to a walkway halfway up the wall – he had been escorted along an identical walkway and down an identical stairway on the opposite wall to his meeting with Treve. He clattered up the stairs and through the hatch into the dimly lit maze beyond.

The dull grey monolith towered overhead, featureless apart from a keyboard and input screen. The chamber rose three storeys high. Something about the way its walls disappeared up into the shadows reminded Martha of a church.

'That's a fabricator?' she asked.

'This is the interface,' Romea replied. 'The fabricator is behind that bulkhead. It's huge.'

As she spoke, the Artificials with whom they had marched through the corridors nodded greetings to those that were already there. While developing their own individual personalities, the Artificials still shared a kind of machine telepathy, through their cybernetic link with the ship's systems, Romea and Edison had explained to her. As soon as the colonists were spotted, moving in force towards the compiler, a cybernetic council of war had taken place and a decision was reached. This had taken a little under three seconds, Edison had added. Imagining how much the Doctor would have enjoyed that last snippet of information, Martha had smiled to herself. The Decision? To reach the compiler first and prevent the colonists activating it, whatever the cost.

'The fabricator makes everything we need to colonise the target world,' Romea said. 'Its database contains design specs for machinery, tools, habitation structures, vehicles… When activated, the fabricator manipulates matter on the molecular level and delivers the finished item to one of five loading bays a thousand metres through there.' Romea pointed at the blank wall to which the interface was bolted.

'Half our number are there,' Edison added. Martha didn't envy the colonists the surprise of finding twenty Edison lookalikes waiting for them. She craned her neck back to look up at the top of the monolith. It certainly made sense – rather than try to pack everything for a centuries-long trip between the stars, just pack a machine that could make everything when you got there. All it needed was a plentiful supply of energy from the sun around which the target world orbited, collected by solar panel arrays the size of Wales. To activate it now, running on stored power in the dark gulf between star systems, would be suicide.

The sight of a face staring down at her from the dark caused her to catch her breath. In the time it took her to shout a warning, the face had become one of many – the colonists, leaping over the rail of a walkway hidden by the shadows, shouting threats as they fell.

The Doctor came to a halt in the middle of a cross-junction. He had the nasty feeling he had been there before.

'Not a good time to get lost,' he muttered.

The dull, ruby glow came from a low-set hatch at the end of one arm of the cross-junction. Inside, banks of flickering lights covering the walls of a hexagonal cubby-hole, a small screen and keyboard. The Doctor watched the lights, noting the patterns that emerged, the patches that remained unlit. The cursor blinked on the screen as it had throughout the centuries this ship had been in flight. He reached for the keyboard, tapped out a staccato rhythm. Reading the response that scrolled across the screen, he broke into a smile.

The sounds of struggle filled the room. Wherever she looked, Martha saw bodies locked in conflict. Ragged blades stabbed and slashed.

'Stop!' she found herself shouting. 'Stop this!'

A colonist and an Artificial, grappling for control of the colonist's jagged blade, collided with Martha, slamming her into the wall. Stars flashed across her vision.

'Martha!' Romea ran towards her… until she was grabbed by the collar of her coverall and jerked backwards, into the arms of a colonist.

Martha shook away the stars and looked up. A colonist stood over her. In his raised fist he held a large spanner.

'Have we met?' Martha asked. The spanner began its descent.

Martha's attacker was slammed aside by an Artificial – Edison? All around her, colonists and Artificials struggled with one another, but suddenly Martha had clear space on every side.

'Stop this!' she shouted again. 'This is bigger than love. Or rules. This is about survival!'

As if in reaction to her words, those fighting all around her stumbled, pressing their hands to their temples or over their ears, shaking their heads, while from above her came a familiar voice:

'Quite right, Martha. Now listen, all of you – Stop. Right now!'

The Doctor's last words brought some of the colonists and Artificials to their knees, hands now firmly clamped over their ears.

On the faces of those nearest to her, Martha could see incomprehension and the beginnings of fear. Looking up, she saw the Doctor, standing on the same walkway from which the colonists had launched their attack. He smiled down at her, then lifted what looked like a microphone to his lips and spoke again.

'Thought that might get your attention. Ladies and Gentlemen, Colonists and… others. I have taken control of the ship.'

An Artificial turned his face towards Martha. A livid bruise covered one half of his forehead and blood ran freely from a lip split in two or three places.

'Your friend…' Martha assumed it must be Edison. The Artificial spoke too loudly, as if shouting to be heard over a noise that Martha couldn't hear. 'He's… in my head. How?'

With a crow-like flapping of his long coat, the Doctor vaulted the walkway rail and landed lightly on his rubber-soled feet a short way from Martha.

'That's a very good question,' he flashed a grin. 'Fortunately, I know the answer.'

From the corner of her eye, Martha caught sight of sudden movement. A colonist staggered to his feet and swung a blunt tool of some sort at the nearest Artificial. Two long strides brought the Doctor within range. Reaching down with his free hand he plucked the tool from the colonist's grasp. Something in the gentle-yet-irresistible nature of the movement reminded her of the way he had prevented the gang of colonists from pursuing Edison down the corridor.

'I said this ends *now*!' the Doctor shouted into the microphone... and every colonist and Artificial in the room clutched at their heads. Some moaned, others cried out. 'In a moment I'm going to turn down the volume. If anyone tries anything nasty, I'll be turning it all the way up to eleven. I can't promise that won't cause permanent damage.' He adjusted something on the stem of the microphone, which Martha thought looked like it had been put together on the run.

With a chorus of relieved sighs and groans, the colonists and Artificials eased themselves off the floor and fell back into two opposing groups, staring warily at each other across the narrow strip of neutral space in which the Doctor and Martha stood. Romea, Martha noticed, stood with the Artificials.

'That's much better. This is for those in the loading bays and anywhere else on board. Just because I'm not there doesn't mean I won't know if you try anything violent, sneaky or otherwise really, really stupid. I am on very good terms with your ship's Pilot System and she is keeping an eye on all of you.'

The Doctor cleared his throat.

'I am speaking to everyone on board the generation ship 374926-slash-GN66 – and by the way, you really should consider coming up with a better name than that – because I want to stop you making the biggest mistake any of you are ever liable to make. To be honest, if you made this mistake it would have to be the biggest because none of you would live to make another one.'

'This is our ship! This is our mission!' Treve was standing at the walkway rail, Laine beside him as he shouted down at the Doctor. They must have been closer behind him than he'd thought. 'Artificials are created to serve and when their purpose is done, to submit and be rendered down for future generations. The purity of the human gene-type must be preserved.' There was a murmur among the colonists. Some shuffled forward.

'Oh, things have gone much, much too far for that.' The Doctor shook his head, then pointed a finger at the feet of the advancing colonists.

'Eleven,' he said, his tone deceptively light as he jiggled the makeshift microphone loosely.

The colonists withdrew.

'You're rational people: scientists, planetary engineers, world-builders. You all know that purity's not how life works. Life, evolution, creativity – they all thrive on variety, diversity, finding new combinations and seeing what happens. Half of you know that's already happened.' The Doctor shot a significant look at the Artificials.

Romea turned to Edison. 'What does he mean?'

Edison seemed unsure how to answer. He exchanged uncertain glances with the other Artificials.

'I… I know!' Romea gasped, eyes suddenly wide. 'I know what happened – and I'm seeing parts of it, flashes. Memories!' She looked at Edison. 'Your memories?'

The Artificial nodded.

'That's a girl!' the Doctor shouted. 'The connection's been there all along. All you have to do is recognise it!'

'I was… I was dying!' Romea stared across at the other colonists. 'We all were!'

A colonist cried out, his face wearing the same wide-eyed expression as Romea. 'I… I see it too!'

There was another cry, then a gasp. Another colonist fell to her knees, sobbing, while another held his hands in front of his face and gazed at them as if they belonged to someone else.

Whatever was affecting the colonists was moving fast, jumping from one to another like a high-voltage charge. There was more weeping. Some of them just stood and shook their heads. Their faces were pictures of despair and wonder.

Martha shot the Doctor a puzzled look.

'The Pilot System explained things,' the Doctor began. 'I ran into her by accident, really. I was on my way here but must have taken a wrong turn around the atmospheric scrubbers. Anyway, I came across a system node and introduced myself.'

'Never mind that I was about to get my head bashed in,' Martha scolded him. But she was smiling.

The Doctor shrugged and returned her smile. 'One look at the surveillance system feed showed me things were getting bad down here. I had to come up with something that would stop everybody killing everybody else. That's when I caught sight of the Pilot's log.

'The Artificials are linked to the Pilot System. Cybernetic grafts performed *in vitro*.' The Doctor tapped the side of his head. 'It's how she wakes them up when it's time for a spot of housekeeping, or if there's a problem on board.'

'Like the cryo-system failing?'

'Exactly. Well, it turns out that the failure was catastrophic. Fatal.'

'We know that. Romea told me the rest. Half the colonists died.'

The Doctor shook his head.

'Not half. All of them.'

There was a sudden clatter from the metal ladder that led to the walkway. Treve had slid from about halfway up. He now clung grimly to the handrail, having regained his balance, but the look in his eyes was wild. Romea ran to him. 'Dad!' she cried softly. 'Oh, Dad.'

'Impossible!' Treve muttered, barely noticing his daughter. 'Impossible!'

'Some people are going to have a hard time getting used to this,' said the Doctor.

'Getting used to what?' Martha asked.

'Being Artificial,' the Doctor told her. 'When the cryo-system crashed, the shock killed a lot of the colonists outright. Others died more slowly. The Pilot System woke all available Artificials to revive the rest, but it was too late. So they did the next best thing: they downloaded the colonists' personality imprints and kicked the Artificial production line into high gear. They used up every last drop of raw material to create bodies for as many of the colonists as they could save. Even used DNA from the colonists' bodies to make sure they looked pretty much as they looked when they went into storage.'

'They grew new bodies for the colonists?' Martha looked from colonists to Artificials and back. Suddenly she was seeing how alike they looked, behind their superficial differences. 'Why didn't they tell them?'

'Thought it might freak them out, so soon after the shock of losing so many of their loved ones. Then, as tensions grew between them, they thought it might provoke violence. Much better that they discover it for themselves.'

'These new bodies have the same cybernetic link as the Artificials?' Martha asked. 'So that's why they could hear you in their heads, too?'

'They didn't know it was there. Your friend Romea was probably more in tune with it. That could be why she was attracted to an Artificial. As for the others, all they needed was a catalyst to get the process started.'

Martha was watching the colonists. They moved slowly, like people waking from a dream. The Artificials moved towards them cautiously, offering support and words of comfort.

'They were about to kill everyone to stop the Artificials acting like people,' she said. 'But everybody's artificial now.'

'Everybody's artificial now,' the Doctor said. 'But love is real.'

'I've been meaning to ask you,' Martha said. There was a distant look in the Doctor's eyes which made her anxious to change the subject. 'Back in the corridor you made some weird-looking moves. And you did it on the guy who tried to kick things off again. Time Lord kung-fu?'

'Amtorian jiu-jitsu.' The faraway look became a smile, as if the Doctor was grateful to have the subject changed. 'Masters of the art vow never to use it in public. Just watching it can do spectators a mischief – headaches, nosebleeds and much worse.'

The Doctor guided Martha away, and they weaved their way towards the door, making their apologies and passing between the groups of Artificials and colonists – though, Martha realised, that distinction had lost all meaning.

'Come on, let's see if I can't give the energy cells an upgrade, make the reserves last long enough to get them where they're going – provided they don't go starting up the fabricator prematurely.' His smile broadened and he spun his sonic screwdriver around one finger, gunslinger-style.

'This Amtorian jiu-jitsu,' Martha said as they reached the door. 'You any good at it?'

'Not bad, actually. I always meant to take my final rank grading – very fetching belt: purple and puce…'

The travellers stepped into the dimly lit corridor. It would be the last time any of the generation ship's passengers would remember seeing them.

'… I just never got around to it. Takes ages, you see, and

takes place any time, anywhere. You can be taking a bath, shopping or just walking down the street when one of the masters jumps out and attacks you…'

They made their way back to the TARDIS, standing in a huge empty cargo space that, Martha hoped, would one day be full of fabricator-made equipment with which the colonists would begin to build a new world – for themselves and for those they once considered merely Artificial.

The Doctor was about to open the TARDIS door when he hesitated, key raised.

'Did you hear…?' he said. His eyes darted this way and that, checking the shadows.

'You did tell the Amtorians you weren't taking that grading, didn't you?' Martha asked.

'Yes! Absolutely. Probably.' The Doctor slotted home the key and pushed the door open a little too urgently for Martha's liking. 'Perhaps… we should be going!'

FIFTEEN

'**W**e are not unsympathetic,' said the Drast. Standing on the observation platform with the Segue slowly flickering below them, the beautiful masked faces of the Drast looked at Martha.

For a moment, she felt a flutter of hope. 'Then you'll help me?' she asked.

'We will not help you,' said one of the Drast.

'But you should not be disheartened,' said another.

'What do you mean?' asked Martha, puzzled.

'Your species will not suffer for very much longer,' said the first Drast.

'As soon as the Segue is successfully calibrated, we will leave this world,' said the second. 'When we leave, we will be obliged to open the Segue more fully.'

'This will cause a catastrophic quantum collapse,' said another. 'It is an unfortunate but necessary consequence of full Segue operation.'

'The Earth will be disintegrated,' another told her. 'The

Master will die.'

'The human race will be put out of its misery and spared a future of suffering.'

'No!' Martha stammered. 'No, no! That's not what I want! I don't want you to kill us all! I don't want you to put us out of our misery! I want you to help us!'

'We thought you would be content,' said the Drast.

'This is what will take place,' said one.

'We consider it favourable,' said another.

Martha took a few steps backwards in shock, too stunned to speak. The enormity of what the Drast had just told her, so clinically and matter-of-factly, began to sink in.

In order to save the world from the Master, she now had to save the world from the Drast.

'Begin the next recalibration test,' the Drast said.

In the chamber below her, the armed guards were leading in the next volunteer.

It was Griffin.

He glanced up at her, but did not acknowledge her. He was busy fiddling with the buckles of his safety harness.

'This is loose,' he told one of the guards. 'I don't want it coming off. Can you tighten the buckle? I can't reach it.'

Griffin glanced up at her again. This time he winked. With a sudden chill, Martha realised that Griffin was about to try something. He was surrounded by guards. The idiot was going to get himself killed. She had to do something. She had to distract them.

'Stop!' she shouted from the platform. 'That man's not a suitable candidate for the Segue!'

The Drast turned to stare at her, questioningly. Down below, the guards faltered and looked up at the platform for clarification. Their attention was no longer focused on Griffin.

One of the guards had moved in to adjust Griffin's harness. As he and the other guards looked up, Griffin ripped out a fist and floored him. At the same moment, Griffin grabbed the trailing safety line and lashed it around like a skipping rope, snagging the other two guards around the knees. With a savage snap of the line, Griffin flipped them both onto their backs. It happened so fast.

Griffin knelt, delivered another vicious punch to make sure the first guard was unconscious, and then took hold of the man's machine gun. As the other two guards attempted to rise, he shot them both at close range.

The whole episode had taken less than four seconds.

Alarms started to sound. The Drast looked down from the platform in dismay.

'What is he doing?' asked one.

'He is deranged,' said another.

'Contain the Segue Chamber,' ordered a third.

'Oh, Griffin, you maniac! What are you doing?' Martha murmured as she stared down into the chamber. More guards were storming into the vault. Griffin had detached his safety line and was rushing towards the obelisk plinth. The guards seemed reluctant to take a shot for fear of hitting the Segue assembly.

'Detain him,' said one of the Drast.

'Disarm him.'

'This is unfavourable.'

Griffin stood on the plinth. He had a predatory grin plastered all over his scarred face. He looked up at the observation platform and yelled, 'You see me? You see me, up there? I'll be honest, I don't know how this thing works!' Griffin aimed his captured machine gun at the one of the obelisks. 'But I'll bet real money that emptying an entire clip into it on full auto is going to be bad news!'

'The test candidate must not be allowed to damage the Segue,' said one of the Drast. Behind their masks, the Drast were glowing brightly, as if in a heightened state.

'Is he right?' Martha demanded. 'What would happen?'

'Concussive, explosive trauma to the Segue assembly could cause Segue generation failure,' said one of the Drast.

'There is also a probability,' said another of the Drast, 'that concussive, explosive trauma to the Segue assembly could trigger a cascade reaction in the Black Hole Converter.'

'And that would mean?' Martha urged.

'This island group would be annihilated in a mass gravitational implosion.'

'Do you hear me?' Griffin yelled. 'Call off your goons and let me and the volunteers out of here, or I'll shoot. I'm not kidding around! What's it going to be?'

'I think you should listen to him,' Martha told the Drast. 'I really think you should.'

'Why?' asked the Drast.

'Because he's one of the most ruthless men I've ever had the misfortune of meeting,' said Martha. 'He absolutely means what he says.'

'This is unfavourable,' the Drast chorused, glowing more brilliantly.

'Don't push him,' warned Martha. 'Shut the Segue down.'

'That is an unfavourable option,' said one of the Drast.

'The Segue is linked to the Zone's primary power grid,' said another.

'So?' asked Martha.

'If we shut the Segue down, it will cause a power blackout across the entire industrial sector.'

'I don't think you've got a lot of choice,' said Martha. 'Unless you want to risk him blowing us all up.'

'A power blackout would collapse our disguise fields,' said one of the Drast.

'It would reveal us to the Master,' said another.

'Well, that's a shame,' said Martha. 'If your disguise fields collapse, you'll have to find a new place to hide. Alternatively, you can die right now.'

'I'm waiting!' Griffin roared.

The Drast looked at one another.

'Initiate Segue shutdown,' the Drast said.

A painful prickle of static filled the air. There was a loud series of bangs as power systems cut off or switched to standby. The lazy lightning bolt of the Segue shivered and then vanished in a belch of gas and overpressure.

Koban plant plunged into blackness.

Kuro, Shiro and the other manufacturing plants went dark. Blackouts overtook the Aka and the other slave camps.

Grid by grid, block by block, Yokohama, Tokyo and the entire bay area went out.

In the first ten minutes of the blackout, panic boiled through the labour zones, the Marine Terminals and the plant domes. After twenty minutes, rioting began. Gunfire was rattling out across the smog-bound megapolis sector. Frantic workers were overwhelming UCF riot squads.

The Drast had fled. Martha never found out what became of them. She suspected that their lives didn't last very long after the shutdown.

Martha moved through the Koban plant. There was no light. With the disguise fields cancelled, her perception filter had started to work again. Frantic guards bumbled past her in the gloom.

She located the holding room, and took off her key. The volunteers were in a state of terrified pandemonium.

'Come on!' she yelled. 'It's me! It's Martha!'

'Listen! It's Martha!' Hito cried.

'I'm going to get you out of here!' Martha shouted. 'Follow me!'

'Martha!' Tokami wailed. 'It is so dark! Are we going to perish?'

'No, we're not!' Martha said. 'Follow me!'

Terror strangled the pitch-black tunnels and hallways of Koban plant. Griffin heard gunfire chattering and booming in the corridors around him. The guards were shooting at anything and everything, even each other.

He hugged the walls, the machine gun in his hands. His

eyes were adapting to the gloom.

Two guards in hazmat suits came racing around a corner ahead of him. He aimed the gun, closed his eyes, and let off a spray of rounds. No point letting muzzle flash destroy his twilight vision.

He checked the corpses, helping himself to spare clips and a pistol. In one bloodstained pocket, he found a mobile phone.

Griffin switched it on. The service finder icon whirled hopelessly, on the bright little screen, for over a minute. Then it stopped, and the icon of the Archangel Network appeared.

Griffin grinned. He'd had the number on his phone for six months. He'd learned it by heart.

SIXTEEN

A serious sense of alarm had begun to spread on the operations deck of HMS *Valiant*.

'Yokohama/Tokyo Zone is not responding,' one operator reported.

'Power reads as down. I've got reports of rioting,' called another.

'This is bad,' said the deck officer, reviewing the reports as fast as they came in. 'This is a disaster. The guidance plants have closed down.'

'Someone will have to tell him,' suggested an aide.

'Not yet! God help us, not yet!' the deck officer exclaimed. 'He'll go ballistic! You know what he gets like when he hears bad news!'

'Shoot the messenger?' the aide said.

'He'd shoot us all,' replied the deck officer. 'Or worse. Why did this have to happen on my watch?' The aide declined to answer. The deck officer turned to the staff manning the operation stations. 'Get me a complete picture. Full spectrum sweep, all the data you can get. Route Toclafane shoals from North Korea and Russia. Wake up UCF Taiwan and find out if they know what the hell's going on. If I've got to report bad news to him, I want it to be the full picture.'

The operations staff got to work. The air became busy with chatter and demands for info.

At her desk, disturbed by the patchy, desperate data coming out of Japan, the ADC jumped when her phone rang. She answered it.

'Griffin, this will have to wait,' she said. 'We've— What? Where are you? Say again? You're *where*? Slow down! Slow down, Griffin… Start at the beginning…'

When she finished the call, she saw a look on the deck officer's face as he read the reports.

'Sir?' she said.

'It's a disaster, ADC,' the deck officer said. 'The guidance plants were a vital resource, and they've gone dark. It's mayhem down there.'

'Do you want me to take this to him?' the ADC asked.

The deck officer looked at the ADC as if she'd just saved his life. She probably had.

'Would you?' he asked.

He was standing on the bridge, in his tailored suit, gazing pensively at the world he had brought to its knees. As tyrants went, and they all went one day, he looked remarkably chipper.

He looked around as the door chimed open. The ADC walked in.

'See?' he smiled. 'My day just got even better. A gorgeous young lady in uniform. Ah, the perks of power.'

'Sir,' the ADC saluted.

He hand-slid down the stair-rails to greet her, a lascivious grin on his face.

'Keep "sir"-ing me like that, and I'll promote you to queen,' he said. 'There must be somewhere that needs a queen. I'll look into it. What have you got for me? Not all bad news, I hope?'

'Some bad news, I'm afraid, sir.'

His face darkened. 'Oh dear,' he said, deflating. 'Not another food riot in Brazil. I hate it when that happens.'

'No, sir,' said the ADC cautiously. 'There's been an incident in Honshu.'

'Honshu? Japanese Honshu? I don't like the sound of that. I've got a lot of interests in Honshu. Show me.'

The ADC handed him the report. He read it over rapidly.

'The whole zone?' he asked. 'The whole zone? All of the guidance plants?'

'Yes, sir. Power has been down for sixty-four minutes, sir.'

He took a deep breath and scratched his forehead. 'I'm really going to be obliged to kill someone about this,' he said.

'I'm certain you are, sir,' the ADC said. 'There is another factor for your consideration.' She handed him another sheet of paper. 'Transcript of a phone conversation I took thirty minutes ago. I thought you'd want to see it.'

He read the sheet.

'The Drast? *The Drast?* Here?' he said. 'Those fortune-hunting, glowy-glowy, entrepreneuring nobodies? The *Drast*? Did you know anything about this?'

His last remark was aimed at the wizened old man sitting in a wheelchair by the window. The wizened old man didn't reply.

'Still, the Drast?' he said, leaning back and cocking his head to one side. 'I'll teach the Drast to mess with me. Bioluminescent idiots. And I was starting to like Japan so much.' He looked at the ADC. 'Calm your pretty head,' he said. 'I'm not angry with you. Who could ever be angry with such a gorgeous thing? Summon the Toclafane swarms. I want the Drast to know, without any qualification, who's Master.'

'Yes, sir.'

He pursed his lips and chewed his jaw to and fro for a moment.

'Burn the islands,' he decided. 'Yes, burn them. We can build guidance somewhere else.'

'Yes, sir.'

He looked at the wizened old man in the wheelchair. The old man's eyes were glaring, hooded by extreme time, painfully disapproving.

'Oh come *on*,' he cried, enthusiastically. 'Vengeance can be so much fun!'

Martha Jones watched, from a container ship leaving the port of Yokohama, as Japan died. Swarms of Toclafane screamed in, unleashing laser death. The cities began to burn.

Knowing that the Master's attention had turned on Japan, knowing that he would be furious about the Drast, Martha had skipped onto the first boat out, unseen, thanks to her perception filter.

She knew she couldn't be anywhere near the Master's focus. The container ship was heading for San Diego. She would make landfall in the USA in a few weeks. In her hurry to escape, Martha had left Hito, Tokami and the other volunteers to cope in the hinterlands behind Koban plant.

She had known the Master would be angry. She had known he would be vindictive. She had hoped he would send forces in to seize and dismantle the Drast plant at Koban.

She had underestimated his venom. She had underestimated it too much.

He wasn't going to be vindictive. He was going to be genocidal.

The islands of Japan burned.

The islands were on fire. Gigantic plumes of flame gushed up out of Tokyo and Chiba. Though the ship was far out at sea, flakes of soot fluttered down onto them.

For the first and only time in her year of walking, Martha allowed herself to cry.

She cried for a long time.

The streets were burning.

Gun in hand, Griffin stumbled out into the open. Smoke was everywhere.

Two Toclafane globes zipped down to meet him.

'I'm clear! I'm UCF!' he shouted. 'I was the one who brought you here! Come *on* now!'

'This person is unidentified,' chuckled one globe.

'Let's kill him,' giggled the other.

'I'm the one!' Griffin yelled. 'I'm the one who brought you in!' He opened his phone. 'ADC? Where's that extraction you promised? I'm in a fix here!'

The hovering Toclafane snapped out their blades.

'That's not soon enough! ADC! For God's sake!'

The globes whirred forwards.

Griffin shrieked.

It felt as if the whole world was made out of night.

Their small boat was racing the swell against an invisible coast. The sky was starless and dark, and the sea was like black glass.

The little outboard motor chugged. The enclosing night was cool, and smelled of brine and Channel breezes. The year was almost up. She had walked the Earth, and witnessed things that she would never forget.

A small, blue-white light appeared in the darkness ahead of them, tiny but stark. It was a halogen lamp, flashing once, twice; a little cold star shining on an unseen beach.

'There!' she said.

The light began to swing, gently, from side to side.

They came in through the breakers, the outboard throbbing. She felt the boat's belly scrape and rumble across the shingle. She got up and jumped out. Cold water sucked at her legs.

She looked back at the men wrangling the small boat. She couldn't see their faces. She wished she could.

She ran up the beach towards the light. Her wet boots crunched over damp sand and pebbles. A young man was waiting for her on the foreshore, a halogen lamp in his hand.

She came up to face him, slightly out of breath.

'What's your name, then?' she asked.

'Tom,' he said. 'Milligan. No need to ask who you are. Famous Martha Jones. How long since you were last in Britain?'

'Three hundred and sixty-five days,' Martha replied. 'It's been a long year.'

Acknowledgements

Dan Abnett would like to thank Justin Richards, Steve Tribe, Gary Russell and Russell T Davies.

David Roden wishes to express his gratitude to: Nikki Smith; Kevin Myers; the brilliant team at BBC Wales; Pauline and Barrie Mansell; and last, but by no means least, particular special thanks must go to Guy Siner, for counsel and comradeship, red wine and being an all-round good egg.

Steve Lockley and Paul Lewis would like to thank Mark Morris for the introduction, and everyone who has made *Doctor Who* the show we know and love.

Robert Shearman's thanks go to Ian Mond and Liz Myers.

Simon Jowett thanks: all the usual suspects for reviving *Doctor Who* with such energy, joy and sheer chutzpah; and Mina, my little girl, for reminding me what it's like to be transfixed, taken over and utterly transported by a piece of cracking Saturday night telly.

DOCTOR · WHO

THE CLOCKWISE MAN
by Justin Richards

THE MONSTERS INSIDE
by Stephen Cole

WINNER TAKES ALL
by Jacqueline Rayner

THE DEVIANT STRAIN
by Justin Richards

ONLY HUMAN
by Gareth Roberts

THE STEALERS OF DREAMS
by Steve Lyons

DOCTOR · WHO

THE STONE ROSE
by Jacqueline Rayner

THE FEAST OF THE DROWNED
by Stephen Cole

THE RESURRECTION CASKET
by Justin Richards

THE NIGHTMARE OF BLACK ISLAND
by Mike Tucker

THE ART OF DESTRUCTION
by Stephen Cole

THE PRICE OF PARADISE
by Colin Brake

Also available from BBC Books
featuring the Doctor and Martha
as played by David Tennant and Freema Agyeman:

DOCTOR · WHO

STING OF THE ZYGONS
by Stephen Cole

THE LAST DODO
by Jacqueline Rayner

WOODEN HEART
by Martin Day

FOREVER AUTUMN
by Mark Morris

SICK BUILDING
by Paul Magrs

WETWORLD
by Mark Michalowski

WISHING WELL
by Mark Morris

THE PIRATE LOOP
by Simon Guerrier

PEACEMAKER
by James Swallow

Also available from BBC Books
featuring the Doctor and Martha
as played by David Tennant and Freema Agyeman:

DOCTOR · WHO

Martha in the Mirror

by Justin Richards

ISBN 978 1 84607 420 2
UK £6.99 US $11.99/$14.99 CDN

Castle Extremis – whoever holds it can control
the provinces either side that have been at war for
centuries. Now the castle is about to play host to the
signing of a peace treaty. But as the Doctor and Martha
find out, not everyone wants the war to end.

Who is the strange little girl who haunts the castle?
What is the secret of the book the Doctor finds, its
pages made from thin, brittle glass? Who is the hooded
figure that watches from the shadows? And what is the
secret of the legendary Mortal Mirror?

The Doctor and Martha don't have long to find the
answers – an army is on the march, and the castle will
soon be under siege once more…

Also available from BBC Books
featuring the Doctor and Martha
as played by David Tennant and Freema Agyeman:

DOCTOR·WHO

SnowGlobe 7

by Mike Tucker

ISBN 978 1 84607 421 9

UK £6.99 US $11.99/$14.99 CDN

Earth, 2099. Global warming is devastating the climate. The polar ice caps are melting.

In a desperate attempt at preservation, the governments of the world have removed vast sections of the Arctic and Antarctic and set them inside huge domes across the world. The Doctor and Martha arrive in SnowGlobe 7 in the Middle East, hoping for peace and relaxation. But they soon discover that it's not only ice and snow that has been preserved beneath the Dome.

While Martha struggles to help with an infection sweeping through the Dome, the Doctor discovers an alien threat that has lain hidden since the last ice age. A threat that is starting to thaw.

DOCTOR·WHO

The Many Hands
by Dale Smith
ISBN 978 1 84607 422 6
UK £6.99 US $11.99/$14.99 CDN

The Nor' Loch is being filled in. If you ask the soldiers
there, they'll tell you it's a stinking cesspool that the
city can do without. But that doesn't explain why the
workers won't go near the place without an armed
guard.

That doesn't explain why they whisper stories about
the loch giving up its dead, about the minister who
walked into his church twelve years after he died…

It doesn't explain why, as they work, they whisper
about a man called the Doctor.

And about the many hands of Alexander Monro.

DOCTOR·WHO

Starships and Spacestations

by Justin Richards

ISBN 978 1 84607 423 3

£7.99 US $12.99/$15.99 CDN

The Doctor has his TARDIS to get him from place to place and time to time, but the rest of the Universe relies on more conventional transport… From the British Space Programme of the late twentieth century to Earth's Empire in the far future, from the terrifying Dalek Fleet to deadly Cyber Ships, this book documents the many starships and spacestations that the Doctor and his companions have encountered on their travels.

He has been held prisoner in space, escaped from the moon, witnessed the arrival of the Sycorax and the crash landing of a space pig… More than anyone else, the Doctor has seen the development of space travel between countless worlds.

This stunningly illustrated book tells the amazing story of Earth's ventures into space, examines the many alien fleets who have paid Earth a visit, and explores the other starships and spacestations that the Doctor has encountered on his many travels…

India in 1947 is a country in the grip of chaos – a
country torn apart by internal strife. When the Doctor
and Donna arrive in Calcutta, they are instantly swept
up in violent events.

Barely escaping with their lives, they discover that the
city is rife with tales of 'half-made men', who roam the
streets at night and steal people away. These creatures,
it is said, are as white as salt and have only shadows
where their eyes should be.

With help from India's great spiritual leader,
Mohandas 'Mahatma' Gandhi, the Doctor and Donna
set out to investigate these rumours.

What is the real truth behind the 'half-made men'?
Why is Gandhi's role in history under threat? And has
an ancient, all-powerful god of destruction really come
back to wreak his vengeance upon the Earth?

DOCTOR·WHO

The Doctor Trap

by Simon Messingham

ISBN 978 1 846 07558 0

UK £6.99 US $11.99/$14.99 CDN

Sebastiene was perhaps once human. He might look
like a nineteenth-century nobleman, but in truth he is
a ruthless hunter. He likes nothing more than luring
difficult opposition to a planet, then hunting them
down for sport. And now he's caught them all – from
Zargregs to Moogs, and even the odd Eternal…

In fact, Sebastiene is after only one more prize. For
this trophy, he knows he is going to need help. He's
brought together the finest hunters in the universe to
play the most dangerous game for the deadliest quarry
of them all.

They are hunting for the last of the Time Lords
– the Doctor.

Also available from BBC Books
featuring the Doctor and Donna
as played by David Tennant and Catherine Tate:

DOCTOR·WHO

Beautiful Chaos

by Gary Russell

ISBN 978 1 846 07563 6

UK £6.99 US $11.99/$14.99 CDN

Donna Noble is back home in London, catching
up with her family and generally giving them all
the gossip about her journeys. Her grandfather is
especially overjoyed – he's discovered a new star and
had it named after him. He takes the Doctor, as his
special guest, to the naming ceremony.

But the Doctor is suspicious about some of the other
changes he can see in Earth's heavens. Particularly
that bright star, right there. No, not that one, that one,
there, on the left…

The world's population is slowly being converted to a
new path, a new way of thinking. Something is coming
to Earth, an ancient force from the Dark Times.
Something powerful, angry, and all-consuming…

DOCTOR · WHO

The Eyeless

by Lance Parkin

ISBN 978 1 846 07562 9
UK £6.99 US $11.99/$14.99 CDN

At the heart of the ruined city of Arcopolis is the Fortress. It's a brutal structure placed here by one of the sides in a devastating intergalactic war that's long ended. Fifteen years ago, the entire population of the planet was killed in an instant by the weapon housed deep in the heart of the Fortress. Now only the ghosts remain.

The Doctor arrives, and determines to fight his way past the Fortress's automatic defences and put the weapon beyond use. But he soon discovers he's not the only person in Arcopolis. What is the true nature of the weapon? Is the planet really haunted? Who are the Eyeless? And what will happen if they get to the weapon before the Doctor?

The Doctor has a fight on his hands. And this time he's all on his own.

Coming soon from BBC Books
featuring the Doctor
as played by David Tennant:

DOCTOR · WHO

Judgement of the Judoon
by Colin Brake
ISBN 978 1 846 07639 8
UK £6.99 US $11.99/$14.99 CDN

Elvis the King Spaceport has grown into the sprawling
city-state of New Memphis – an urban jungle, where
organised crime is rife. But the launch of the new
Terminal 13 hasn't been as smooth as expected. And
things are about to get worse...

When the Doctor arrives, he finds the whole terminal
locked down. The notorious Invisible Assassin is at
work again, and the Judoon troopers sent to catch him
will stop at nothing to complete their mission.

With the assassin loose on the mean streets of New
Memphis, the Doctor is forced into a strange alliance.
Together with teenage private eye Nikki and a ruthless
Judoon Commander, the Doctor soon discovers that
things are even more complicated – and dangerous –
than he first thought…

DOCTOR·WHO

The Slitheen Excursion

by Simon Guerrier

ISBN 978 1 846 07640 4

UK £6.99 US $11.99/$14.99 CDN

1500BC – King Actaeus and his subjects live in mortal fear of the awesome gods who have come to visit their kingdom in ancient Greece. Except the Doctor, visiting with university student June, knows they're not gods at all. They're aliens.

For the aliens, it's the perfect holiday – they get to tour the sights of a primitive planet and even take part in local customs. Like gladiatorial games, or hunting down and killing humans who won't be missed.

With June's enthusiastic help, the Doctor soon meets the travel agents behind this deadly package holiday company – his old enemies the Slitheen. But can he bring the Slitheen excursion to an end without endangering more lives? And how are events in ancient Greece linked to a modern-day alien plot to destroy what's left of the Parthenon?

Coming soon from BBC Books
featuring the Doctor
as played by David Tennant:

DOCTOR·WHO

Prisoner of the Daleks

by Trevor Baxendale

ISBN 978 1 846 07641 1

UK £6.99 US $11.99/$14.99 CDN

The Daleks are advancing, their empire constantly expanding into Earth's space. The Earth forces are resisting the Daleks in every way they can. But the battles rage on across countless solar systems. And now the future of our galaxy hangs in the balance…

The Doctor finds himself stranded on board a starship near the frontline with a group of ruthless bounty hunters. Earth Command will pay them for every Dalek they kill, every eye stalk they bring back as proof.

With the Doctor's help, the bounty hunters achieve the ultimate prize: a Dalek prisoner – intact, powerless, and ready for interrogation. But where the Daleks are involved, nothing is what it seems, and no one is safe. Before long the tables will be turned, and how will the Doctor survive when he becomes a prisoner of the Daleks?